# Alexander the Good Dragon

Romans 8:28

# Alexander
## The Good Dragon

## by Fred Wolf

### cover illustration by Steve Wolf

ISBN-13: 978-0-692-44161-9


First Printing

Requests for information should be addressed to:

Fred Wolf
P.O. Box 213
New Melle, MO 63365


Cover illustration by Steve Wolf
http://www.wolfcreativeusa.com

Typesetting by Eric Fritzius
http://www.mrherman.com


**http://www.alexanderthegooddragon.com**


*Alexander the Good Dragon* is a work of fiction. Names, characters, places, and incidents are a product of the author's imagination or are used fictitiously. Any resemblance to actual persons living or dead, events, or locales is entirely coincidental.

**To the King of all kings,**
**who slew the dragon two thousand years ago.**

*This story takes place in England*
*centuries and centuries and centuries ago,*
*before the great serpents died off.*
*A time when kings ruled the earth*
*and dragons ruled the skies ...*

# Prologue

Alexander awoke when the first beams of sunlight fell across his eyelids. He opened his eyes, which burned orange and glittered with gold that glowed like flaming tungsten. As he rose from the cave's cold floor and stretched his forelegs, black talons scraped the stone. Then he arched his back like a cat, and a pair of massive wings unfurled. Their tips brushed the stalactites above.

He froze. The impression in the dust on the stone floor where his mate Evangeline slept beside him remained empty, although her scent lingered. Long strides carried Alexander to the mouth of the cave and out into the sun. His pupils narrowed to slits, and the small forest-green scales that pebbled his face gleamed. The clear blue sky stretched across the mountains and forests below, but the brisk air carried an odor that sent a bolt of fear through Alexander. Decay.

Alexander lunged forward down the mountain path that led to his lair. The ground trembled under the impact of his pounding feet, and his shoulders rocked back and forth with each rhythmic stride. Soon the rushing air pressed up under his wings, and he spread them wide. Then, gathering his haunches beneath him, the dragon launched into the air and pumped his massive wings. The rocky mountain fell away

1

beneath him, and his deep chest heaved as his shadow swept across the forest below, sending a herd of deer sprinting into the trees.

Alexander glided toward a gap in the trees, where a quiet lagoon reflected the sun like a mirror. But something else was reflecting the morning light. It was then that Alexander spied his mate's pearly skin as she lay on the bank of the lagoon where she bathed each morning. He tilted his wings and swept down toward her, but as he neared, a cold tremor ran through him. Evangeline lay on her side, her long body curled in the fetal position. Turquoise eyes remained open and glazed, and saliva pooled beneath her slack jaws. A pile of silvery-pink salmon – some half-eaten – spilled across the ground alongside her body.

Alexander's huge feet hit the ground hard. He galloped forward to Evangeline's body, slowed, and nudged her iridescent neck with the bridge of his nose. Her body heat was fading, and her eyes stared out like those of the fish before her, wide and unblinking.

She had been alive the night before, even that morning, stepping into the sunlight and opening her wings to absorb the warmth. Alexander had watched from the floor as the sunlight illuminated her translucent membranes, making them glow a faint cream color. She had returned to him before she left to run her smooth neck across his, a rumble throbbing in her throat. The vibrations had passed through her skin and into his.

Now Alexander's sides pulsed with rapid breaths, and a sour knot gripped his stomach. As he ran his flared nostrils across her sunken flesh, a whine quivered in his throat. Then he sat back, his head spinning with the reek of oil and something else he did not recognize. Alexander sat staring at his mate's body for a few minutes, the birds chirping in the forest around him.

He threw back his head and bellowed to the sky. The sound swept across the lagoon, startling a flock of geese into the air, then continued into the forest. After several seconds, the bellow dropped to a guttural rumble as he emptied his lungs. Several silhouettes silently emerged from beyond the trees and followed the mournful sounds to their leader—and, in most cases, their father, uncle, or grandfather. Each dragon landed along the rocky bank and approached Evangeline's corpse with his own quavering whine. A few curled up close to Alexander, and one disappeared into the forest to return with a small deer for breakfast. None touched the fish.

As the morning passed, a strong breeze moved across the lagoon, but Alexander continued to mourn, lying prostrate near Evangeline's body.

With the nearby deer carcass stripped to its bones, Alexander's mouth watered at the sight of the red meat inside the half-eaten chunk of fish. He rose and leaned over to pluck it from the ground, but his son, Gabriel, darted toward him with a shrill cry. Alexander let out a sharp growl, but the young dragon raked his talons across the fish's scales, spraying rank oil across the pebbles. As drops landed near Alexander's talons, a bitter scent tickled his nostrils.

He remembered that smell; it often tainted the chunks of meat that were scattered here and there in the forest nearby. He had once seen a fox eat the meat and then arch its back and retch until it slumped to the ground. Thinking twice about eating the sick animal, Alexander had left it panting on its side. When he returned hours later, its bloody carcass lay amidst the stained pine needles, its fiery pelt gone. Now the great dragon fixed his eyes on the fish, and caught a whiff of something that reminded him of the dead fox.

Alexander inspected the edge of the forest, his nose to the ground. He raised his mighty head and his snarl tore the air. The strange smell brought back the memory of a tall man Alexander had once seen running into the forest with a large sack. Alexander had circled around and swept low across the treetops, scanning beneath the canopy for the man, but to no avail. A piercing cry from the mountains had distracted Alexander, and he had followed them to a spire where a dragoness crouched over her nest. In it, her offspring's lifeless bodies lay crushed, their throats torn open.

As Alexander moved forward to console the dragoness, a scent reached him through that of the coppery blood. The reek was peppery and acidic: another dragon, and one Alexander recognized. He rushed out of the den, but the offending dragon's black silhouette already shrank on the horizon—and on its back clung the man with the sack. The pair continued north along the Cumbrian Mountain Range while Alexander clung to the mountain's ledge and bellowed. Without enough dragons in his force, he could not follow them to the castle and the woman who led them. The dragons that guarded the castle had already chased Alexander away once, and though he towered over them, they outnumbered him.

Alexander had since learned of the woman in the castle—Lady Silver—and her dragon Nafaar. In recent years, Alexander and several other dragons had responded to distress calls from besieged cities and coal mines to defend them from Lady Silver's dragons. The king kept peace with Alexander and his dragons, and in turn, the dragons defended the cities against Lady Silver. Nafaar often led the attacking dragons, and Alexander recognized the black dragon by the silver-plated spike that protruded from his forehead.

Now Alexander looked down at the half-eaten chunk of fish and remembered the slain dragon offspring, the man's sweat and Nafaar's acrid scent, the tainted meat and the bloody fox. With a growl, Alexander filled his lungs and blasted a cry. As he dug a hole in the pebbled shore and swept the fish into it, the air shook with the beating wings of his dragon force. The violent rush of air combined with the wind to roil the water in the lagoon.

Turning away from his mate's body, Alexander bounded along the shore until his outstretched wings lifted him into the air. The two dozen dragons he'd gathered and raised over the years followed him into the sky, and as he cleared the treetops, Alexander turned north.

* * * *

The dragons flew until the sun sank beneath the horizon. Storm clouds rolled in the sunset's wake, their bellies streaked with crimson and indigo. As thunder echoed across the mountains and the moon rose, Lady Silver's castle appeared in the distance. The sight sent a surge of hot anger through Alexander, and he beat his wings harder.

As the dragons neared the castle, the top of one turret shifted. Scales gleamed in the moonlight, and a silver spike glistened on the dragon's forehead. Alexander dropped his head and roared, the sound echoing down along the castle walls. Nafaar released a drawn-out shriek before dropping off the turret and swooping up toward Alexander. As they met under the clouds, Alexander's dragons surrounded them. The two dragons spat streams of fire at each other, but soon the rolling clouds split open and snuffed their fire. As the rain pelted the dragons, bolts of lightning lit the castle, and the crashing thunder made Alexander's wings vibrate.

A cacophony of screeches rose from the castle behind Nafaar as his dragons rose from the shadows like huge bats. Alexander's dragons dove forward to meet them, their wings glistening like wet leather. As the forces collided, Alexander's dragons loomed over their smaller but more numerous opponents. Alexander's son, Gabriel, joined forces with a larger cousin to seize an attacking opponent. Their talons pierced the squealing animal's flesh, and blood sprayed them as they sent the dragon plummeting to the forest below.

As Gabriel glided away from his cousin, a shadow fell over him as a larger dragon swept down, aiming for the base of his skull. As it dropped, the spines along the young dragon's vertebrae sprang up like quills, and before the descending dragon could veer away, the spines pierced its chest and stomach. A neurotoxin flooded the attacker's veins, and it fell to earth in a ball of spasms and pain.

In the midst of the fighting, a blinding lightning bolt flashed through the sky and struck a pair of dragons tangled by their own talons. The deafening crack drove the other dragons back, and they snorted as the reek of ozone filled the air. They watched the glowing corpses as they fell, smoke trailing behind them. While Alexander looked away, Nafaar dove forward and aimed his talons for his opponent's throat. But the majestic dragon twisted his upper torso out of the way and, as the black dragon rushed past, used his own momentum to lunge down after Nafaar. His talons punched through the hard scales on Nafaar's back and dug into the sinewy muscles.

The black dragon let out an ear-splitting squeal and rolled over, but the roll jerked Alexander out of the way of Nafaar's talons as the pair tumbled toward the earth. Alexander brought his hind legs up and braced his feet against Nafaar's pelvis, then used the momentum of the roll to kick the black dragon toward the ground as it rushed up at them. Nafaar's wings jerked and twitched as the talons sliced out of his back, and Alexander spread his wings in time to catch the air and swoop away.

Nafaar slammed into the earth. A sheet of mud spilled over everything before him, and the impact sent tremors through the ground. Nafaar's dragons drew back from their opponents and shrieked to their leader who lay crumpled in a small crater, where rain mixed with the blood seeping from the deep lacerations along his back. With a few final cries, his dragons broke away and retreated to the castle.

Alexander's chest heaved as he hovered over the broken bodies in the mud. Fourteen of Nafaar's, six of his. Blood ran from torn throats and wings slashed to ribbons. The poisoned dragon still twitched with bloody flecks of foam on its jaws, and a few dragons in the air still bled from deep bites and gashes.

With heavy wings, Alexander turned south. By the time he reached the lagoon, pain radiated across his shaking wings and chest as he glided down toward Evangeline's body, scattering several small animals. Her corpse glowed opal in the moonlight. His aching shoulders throbbed as he draped one wing across her body, exhaled, and closed his eyes.

# Chapter One

An unusually cold autumn arrived in northwest England; leaves fell in a cascade of burnt orange, red, and yellow. Steel gray clouds covered the skies for most of October, but on this day, the clear sunset reflected the same colors as the leaves.

At the southwestern edge of the tiny seaside village of Maryport, Sean Delbridge stood alone in the large room that served as the living, dining, cooking, and bathing room. Steam rose from the water in the large basin beside him, water he had retrieved half an hour ago from the copper boiler in the corner.

Sean stripped off his muddy clothes and stepped into the basin, his legs flushing from the heat. He picked up the floating rag and spent the next minutes scrubbing his skin, shivering and wincing as he washed his sunburned shoulders and face. The basin water turned murky with dirt and sweat, but Sean dipped the rag back into it and wrung it out over his soft brown hair. When he finished, Sean dragged the basin to the side where his mother would use it to wash the floors.

Patting himself dry and putting on a fresh long night shirt, Sean carried his bundled clothes up the stairs and set them beside his bed. Then he slid under the covers, grateful for their warmth. As he rolled onto his side and closed his eyes, a door opened in the hallway. Footsteps entered his room.

"You worked hard today," his father said, his deep voice soft.

The bed shifted and creaked as Sean's father sat. Before Sean could roll over and look up at his father, however, the bleating of their sheep reached the small bedroom window. The sound came from the courtyard between the house and the barn—and Sean had not closed the gate to the pasture. His father sighed.

"Sean, you forgot to close the gate. The sheep could go astray. Go lead them back and close the gate."

Sean's muscles ached, and blissful slumber drew near. He was unwilling to leave the warmth and comfort of his bed. Plus, his mother's ham and vegetable stew still warmed his full stomach. Squeezing his eyes shut, Sean lay motionless.

After a few seconds, his father sighed again. "I hope you are asleep, son. I will do it this time, but be more careful."

His father's boots thumped out of the room and down the stairs. Sean rolled over and sighed as the front door shut. As his mother climbed the stairs and walked to his parents' bedroom, Sean burrowed into his covers like a caterpillar in its cocoon.

His father's scream jolted him like an electric shock. Sean threw back the covers and sprang out of bed, pulling on his trousers. His pounding heart sent a wave of heat through him despite the chill, and his hair stood on end. As he ran into the hallway, he almost collided with his mother, and their brown eyes met for a moment. Then Sean barreled down the stairs and out the door.

Running barefoot through the grass, Sean neared his father's cries. Then another sound reached him, a great thrumming. Moonlight spilled across the field, and Sean stumbled to a stop. In the sky above him dangled his father's silhouette in the talons of a massive dragon. He wriggled and kicked like a mouse in the clutches of an owl. Sean's mother screamed and ran forward.

"Mac! No!"

Her horrified cries startled Sean out of his paralysis. He ran after the dragon, fighting the powerful gusts from its pumping wings that swept his shouts away. Even when the dragon gained enough altitude to lift Mac out of reach, Sean ran until his legs throbbed and he gasped for air. As the dragon rose over the trees beyond the field, Sean slowed to a stop and panted, his hair matted to his forehead. Moonlight flashed against the dragon's talons and a metallic spike on its forehead. Mac's cries trailed off into the distance, and Sean stood shaking in the cold.

# Chapter Two

Sean and his mother ran back to the house to grab their coats and shoes, and then ran into the village for help. The pair pounded on doors and pleaded with anyone who would listen, but the neighbors retreated back into their homes.

"Those are Lady Silver's dragons," an older woman with gray hair said. "We will never be able to stop them. Besides, if we try, she will kill us!"

Some neighbors told them to see Constable Hardy, and others referred them to Vicar Perry. Within minutes, Constable Hardy rushed down the lane, pushing his night shirt down his woolen trousers and carrying his boots under his arm. He stopped in front of Sean and his mother, dropped his boots, and shoved each foot into them. Then, breathing hard, he ran a hand over his dark hair and looked at Sean's mother.

"What is it, Cynthia?"

"Mac's gone, Constable! A dragon took him!" Her high voice broke, and tears streamed down her face. "What do we do?"

Sean shivered under his coat and gazed at his mother, not sure what to do. He turned to the constable. "Can we get word to the king?"

"Of course, Sean." The constable glanced at the sky. "Are you sure it was a dragon?"

Sean nodded anxiously.

Constable Hardy looked back to Sean. "I will send a message to the king. But please, take your mother home and look after her. I will let you know if I hear anything."

Sean and his mother returned to their dark home, lit only by the flickering flames in the fireplace. Sean climbed the stairs with sore feet, and when he reached the top, his mother pulled him to her and sobbed into his shoulder. Sean hesitated for a moment, and then hugged her back. After a few seconds, she released him and walked down the hallway to her bedroom.

Sean heard the sheep bleating outside, his eyes half-closed. Then he turned and crawled into bed where he lay tense and shaking for hours. Only when the birds chirped outside could he no longer keep his eyes open.

\* \* \* \*

When Sean awoke, a low ceiling of clouds crawled across the sky past his window, and it began to rain as the sheep grazed in the courtyard below. Still there. Sean sank back against his pillow with a sigh.

*Papa.*

The memory hit Sean: his father scolding him, his screams as he dangled from the dragon's talons. Sean leaped from his bed and, struggling against the spinning room, ran down the stairs. *Perhaps the previous night had only been a nightmare.* But his mother sat alone at the table, her eyes red and swollen. She hugged a thick wool blanket around her, and on the table sat a Bible and a cup of tea. Sean sat down beside her and looked at her. "Try not to worry, Mama."

As she nodded, the sheep's bleating reached him again. His father's words resurfaced in his mind, and tears stung his eyes. *Papa. It was all my fault.* Sean looked around at the glowing coals in the fireplace, the wandering sheep in the courtyard out the window, his tear-streaked mother. He fidgeted for a few seconds, and then turned to his mother.

"Mama, I know you won't like this, but I have to find Papa. I have to do something, because this is my fault."

His mother gasped. "Oh, don't be foolish, Sean! You have no business feeling guilty. No one blames you for this," She squeezed his hands. "Besides, your father could be a hundred kilometers away by now. That is, if he's still—"

"He is still alive, Mama. I know it!"

A knock at the front door made them jump. Sean pictured his father on the other side, covered in mud and leaves but alive.

Knocking over his chair, Sean ran to the door and flung it open, and his shoulders sank. Vicar Perry stood on the front stoop, his chestnut-colored hair damp from the light rain.

"I'm so sorry to disturb you and your mother, Sean," the vicar said. "I heard what happened and came to see if the church can help you in any way."

"Thank you, but I don't know how you could."

"I understand. I wonder if your mother might see me for a few moments. Perhaps I could pray with you both."

Sean nodded and led him inside. Cynthia stepped forward.

"It is very kind of you to come to our home, Vicar," she said, her voice heavy. "I am afraid Sean and I are in poor spirits, though. But, please, have a cup of tea with us."

The vicar took her hands and squeezed them. "I appreciate that," he said. While the vicar rubbed the chill from his hands, Sean pulled several logs out of a copper barrel in the corner of the room and stacked them in the fireplace; then arranged three chairs in front of it.

"Please have a seat."

"Thank you, Sean."

As the rain pattered against the window panes, Sean poured three he fresh tea, and white steam curled from the cups.

blew on his tea, and then took a sip. "Can you share pened last night, Cynthia?"

15

"Mac's gone. A dragon …" Her voice broke. She put a hand over her mouth and motioned to Sean. As Sean described the events, the vicar frowned.

"Could you see what color the dragon was?"

The image of the dragon appeared in Sean's mind: its gleaming talons, its flashing spike. "Dark gray or black. Its talons and something on its forehead gleamed too, like metal."

Vicar Perry frowned again. "I'm sure you've both heard the stories of colliers and other men disappearing. There's a strong rumor that Lady Silver uses these men to harvest the coal in her mine in the mountains."

Sean remembered his parents whispering about Lady Silver, his father scowling and his mother pale. "Why would she care about coal?"

"She wants power. Our greatest industry is coal, and our economy depends upon it. Whoever controls the coal controls England. So, Lady Silver sends out her dragons to snatch up colliers and then stations the dragons at collieries to prevent new men from working."

"What happens to the mines?" Sean asked.

"Because of the dragons, the colliery's owners have no choice but to shut down mine production. If Lady Silver's plan works, she will control all of England's access to coal. Then she could demand the crown in exchange for access to the coal, and without competition, she could charge a premium price."

16

Sean's mother shook her head. "But Mac was—Mac is a farmer, not a collier."

"I know, Cynthia, but Lady Silver just wants as many laborers as possible."

Sean imagined his father in a mine, although he was not sure what they looked like. He imagined his father hunched over for hours, swinging at the stone walls, wincing and stopping to gasp for air. A sour pang of guilt made him lower his tea.

Cynthia sat up. "Why doesn't Alexander stop them?"

"The one they call the king's dragon?" Sean asked.

Vicar Perry looked at Sean. "Yes, Sean. The greatest dragon in all of England. A majestic creature; dark emerald green with gold scales splashed across his chest. The only dragon big enough and with an army powerful enough to fight Lady Silver's dragons." He looked back at Cynthia. "But nobody has seen Alexander since his mate died, since the battle with Nafaar."

Sean sighed. *"Who?"*

His mother patted his arm without taking her eyes off the vicar, who continued. "Either Alexander died of his wounds, or his mate's death drove him into depression. Most people think Lady Silver plotted his mate's death as well.

"Why would she want to do that? Would that not make him angry?" Sean asked.

The vicar nodded. "Or send him into a depression and sap away his motivation."

17

Sean's mother looked down, her lip trembling. Sean stared at Vicar Perry. "Depressed? Aren't dragons just big lizards?"

The vicar smiled softly. "No, Sean. From what I hear, they are much more intelligent than most animals. More like us, too." He sipped his tea, then wrapped his hands around the warm cup. "Without Alexander to stop her, Lady Silver could continue kidnapping colliers and other men, shut down England's mines, and take over whether by the people's demand for coal or by the force of her dragons."

"But Nafaar is their leader, and Alexander killed him." Sean's mother said. The vicar hesitated, and she covered her mouth. "You think Nafaar took my husband, don't you?"

Glancing at Sean, Vicar Perry took a deep breath and looked back at Cynthia. "From what I understand, Lady Silver's dragons have silver-plated talons ... but only one has a spur on his forehead."

Her face crumpled as a fresh sob burst from her lips. The vicar placed a comforting hand on her shoulder. "Cynthia, I do believe Mac is more valuable alive as one of Lady Silver's laborers than not. At least we have that to hope for."

"What can we do then?" she whispered.

Setting down his tea, Sean stood. "I can't just sit here waiting for Papa to return."

His mother motioned for him to sit down. "I already told you, Sean, I need you here. I should not have to worry about a dragon stealing you too."

"I agree with your mother, Sean," Vicar Perry said. "Lady Silver and Nafaar are too dangerous, and the king must have a plan to rescue these men."

"I'm sorry, but at the very least, I must find Alexander and see if he can help."

Vicar Perry looked at Sean's mother and smiled. "Cynthia, if Sean's resolve is from God—and it may very well be—finding Alexander would be a great step toward ending this crisis. But Sean, if you do not find Alexander, you need to come home."

Sean's mother wiped her eyes. "I knew the day would come when I would have to let you go. I just never thought it would be this soon and under these circumstances. I will pray for your protection." A faint smile crossed her face. "Something tells me I will not sleep much."

"I think a word of prayer would be good here," Vicar Perry said.

They took one another's hands and bowed their heads.

"God, we ask for Your help," the vicar said. "We pray You guide Sean's steps and grant him protection and wisdom. We pray no weapon formed against the Delbridge family will prosper. We ask this in the great name of Jesus. Amen."

As the vicar rose, Sean's mother hugged him. "Thank you so much for coming, Vicar," she said with a weak smile. "And thank you for your prayer. Do you need an umbrella for your ride back into town?"

"No thank you, I have the covered carriage."

Before they reached the front door, Sean asked, "How will I find Alexander?"

Vicar Perry turned around. "His lair is in the highest peak at the southern end of the Cumbrian Mountains." He paused for a moment, and then added, "Visit my friend Micah first. He may be able to help you or at least give you a detailed map of where Alexander lives."

"Who is he?"

The vicar folded his arms and smiled. "He has preached the gospel in every corner of England, and he has always been friends with Alexander."

Sean's eyes bulged. *Friends with a dragon?*

The vicar grinned. "He has visited Maryport several times over the years. I traveled to see him only once, when I needed advice—and Micah did not disappoint me. He lives in a grotto. He is a kind man, and I believe he will give you godly direction in more ways than one."

"Where can I find him?"

"He lives along a stream a few kilometers south of Keswick. No more than a day and a half from here. Just follow the stream, and you will not miss the mouth of his grotto on the west side. Tell him I sent you."

"Do you think Prince can make the journey?" Sean's mother asked Sean.

Sean rubbed his forehead. "He will have to do. I have no other choice."

"I wish I could provide a better horse, but mine is no younger," Vicar Perry said.

Sean walked to the door. "Thank you anyway, Vicar."

As they reached the door, Vicar Perry patted Sean on the arm and walked out onto the porch. The rain had slowed to a drizzle, and sunlight now poked through the clouds.

"God be with you, Sean."

# Chapter Three

The next morning, as Sean's mother prepared a hearty breakfast and a knapsack full of food for the trip, Sean went back upstairs to get his father's sword and scabbard. He threaded his belt through the scabbard's loop, and then placed it along the side of his right leg. In the theatre of his mother's mind, a sword battle would reduce her to sobs. Sean put on his long coat and walked back downstairs.

"Will you not get hot in that coat, dear?" his mother asked.

"I'm fine, Mama," Sean replied, discreetly positioning the sword under his coat as he sat down to a full plate of eggs, cold ham, and bread.

"Well, it should get you through most of the day. I packed enough food for three days, but you should be back before then, don't you think?"

Her voice came out tense, and Sean stuffed a forkful of egg into his mouth so he could avoid answering her. *How can I convince Alexander to help me find Papa? Why would a dragon care about people?* But Lady Silver had her dragons, so perhaps the king had dragons too. And if Alexander confronted Lady Silver, he would also lead Sean to his father.

The plan gave Sean a rush. As he stood from the table, his mother tucked a strand of light brown hair behind her ear, then patted Sean's shoulder and walked him to the door. They pulled on their coats, and she helped him put on his knapsack. When he turned around, her red-rimmed eyes gleamed with unspilled tears.

Sean remembered hearing her crying from her bedroom the previous night, and now she had to let her son go too. Despite the tug of impatience, the thought of leaving her all alone to take care of herself and their home made Sean reach out and hug her.

"Mama, I have to do this. I will come home as soon as I can."

She squeezed him, then let go and wiped her eyes with the back of her hand. Sean opened the door to a gust of cold air, and as he stepped onto the front stoop, the bleating of sheep met him. He stopped and sighed.

"Don't worry about the gate, sweetheart," his mother said, stepping outside and closing the door behind her. "I will take care of it while you get Prince."

A few minutes later, Sean returned with their brown horse, his supplies tied to the saddle. Clutching her coat against her, his mother hurried back from the courtyard and patted the horse's firm neck. Then, she took Sean's hands, bowed her head, and whispered a quick prayer. Sean closed his eyes, but he did not hear her words.

*What if I never find Alexander? Should I come back?* The image of the massive black dragon appeared in his mind. What if he *did* find Alexander? *If he attacks me, what will happen to Mama and Papa?*

His mother's pat on the back snapped Sean back into the moment. He pulled himself up into the squeaky leather saddle, took the reins, and with one last smile at his mother, he nudged Prince with his heels. The horse strode forward until it broke into a canter, then a gallop. Soon, only the wind rushing past his exposed ears and Prince's rhythmic hoof beats filled Sean's mind. His heart sank when he thought about his mother sitting alone at the table waiting for him. But Sean was resolute; he would not return home until he found his father.

# Chapter Four

The rolling Cumbrian Mountains stretched toward the sky as Sean travelled southeast toward Keswick. Every so often, the sun broke through the clouds, and a handful of singular shafts touched the landscape. If Heaven changed seasons, it could not possess more vivid autumn colors than what Sean saw that afternoon.

Sean's family did not use Prince to carry packs or people over long distances, so Sean did not push Prince too hard. Along the way, the path took Prince splashing through half-frozen streams, his blunt hooves splintering the ice with the sound of cracking eggshells. By the time they reached the tiny village of Keswick late that afternoon, Sean's shoulders and neck ached.

Keswick included a few dozen houses surrounded by open fields and forest. Prince slowed to a languid walk, and after having ridden alone for hours, Sean smiled at the people he passed. A girl with long blonde hair stared for a moment, then blushed and looked down. The clang of a blacksmith echoed from around the corner, and when the breeze shifted, it brought the aroma of fresh bread from a nearby bakery. Sean's stomach growled, but he had neither the time nor money to spare. He had to find Micah's grotto before sunset.

After Sean asked a man his father's age for directions, Sean led Prince to the stream just outside the village and followed alongside it. The sky glowed citrus, but the setting sun pulled the yellow and orange beneath the horizon, and soon only crimson and indigo remained—a bleeding, bruised sky. Sean thought about his father and nudged Prince into a canter.

As the last sliver of sun disappeared below the hills, the wind whipped about Sean, biting his already scarlet ears. He threw a knit scarf around his neck, then rubbed his shoulders as he looked down the stream's rocky bed and the grassy banks above it. He had seen massive paw prints in the mud beside the stream and knew better than to bed down in the open forest. If he did not find Micah's grotto before sunset, he had to find shelter soon.

*Papa, I wish you were here. You would know where to find shelter.*

Sean followed the water's edge into a valley under the forest's thick canopy. As Prince immersed them both in the shadows, the colors around them faded to black and white. Sean squinted to see around him, but the details in his vision shrank until he could only make out the flashing stream and Prince's neck and head in front of him. His hair stood on end, and he pulled himself down close to Prince, who flattened his ears and snorted.

At the base of a bluff, a long shadow revealed a narrow horizontal crevice. Sean pulled Prince as close to the bluff as possible before dismounting. For a moment, he almost expected an animal to explode from the bushes and leap at him. He froze, pressing himself against Prince's quivering shoulder. The horse radiated heat and musk, and its sweat made Sean's own arm slick. He grimaced and pulled away, rubbing his arm on his knapsack's strap. Then, he unclasped his sword and pulled it out, waving the shining blade before him. His pounding heart slowed.

Sean walked to the bluff and found the opening of a small cave. As he held his sword in front of him, he eased into the cave and found just enough room to lie down and insulate himself from the cold wind. *But what about Prince? Will his sweat attract wolves, bears?* Prince could not fit in the cave, but Sean looked back at the horse standing exposed by the stream. The stream lay below eye level, so nothing could see Prince from the surrounding forest. Sean pulled a bundle of rope from his knapsack—one could always use plenty of rope—and tied Prince to a tree by the stream. After Sean removed the worn saddle, reins, and metal bit, Prince tossed his head and wiggled his stiff mouth. Then the horse lowered his head to rip up tufts of grass.

As Prince grazed, Sean gathered tinder and built a fire just outside the cave. The flames warmed his wind-bitten face and cast its light into the stream and the shallow cave. Sean sat close enough to sear his arms as he heated and then ate his mother's kidney pie, relishing the rich taste of kidney, onion, and salty gravy.

27

With the darkness thickening around him, Sean washed the dish and metal pan in the stream, then retrieved the two blanket rolls tied to his saddle. He carried the blankets and his knapsack into the cave and curled up, resting his head on the hard, bumpy knapsack. He could not wait to get home to his soft, warm bed. As the wind howled through the valley, the flames flickered but never died. Prince clambered up onto the bank and to the fire, stretching his tether until it was almost taut, and lay down. As Sean stared into the monochromatic forest beyond Prince, glowing spheres flashed here and there—eyes reflecting the firelight. But the eyeshine remained far from the stream, and Prince did not stamp his feet or snort as he often did when an animal passed near his stall.

As Sean closed his eyes, a hollow feeling spread through his chest. He had never gone to bed without his parents bidding him a good night's rest. And before the warmth of his blankets lulled him to sleep, Sean prayed for his family.

\* \* \* \*

In the northernmost reaches of the Cumbrian Mountains, a legion of armed guards prowled the huge colliery where kidnapped men shivered as they tried to sleep. With only a single blanket to keep each man from freezing to death, Mac wondered if the flimsy material's only design was not to keep them warm but to provide the minimum insulation needed to keep them from getting sick—and, in doing so, ensuring they could work at the first light of dawn. Thoughts of his beloved Cynthia and Sean allowed Mac to drift into a few hours of sleep while his fellow captives moaned around him.

\* \* \* \*

The next morning, a gray fortress of clouds held the sun at bay over the Cumbrian Mountains, and the wind blew through the trees with a biting cold. Sean might have slept all day had it not been for the incessant caw of a raven circling above the woods. When he awoke, Sean forgot where he was, and the sight of the dank rock ceiling above him made his breath catch. When he remembered his missing father, his chest grew heavy and hollow with dread.

Sean rolled out of his makeshift bed, stood, and stepped out into the muted daylight. His campfire's embers still smoked, so he smothered them with a few handfuls of dirt. As he walked over to where Prince grazed, he noticed chafing sores on the horse's back and belly, as well as the horse's swollen knees.

Sean laid his saddle across the horse's back but left the straps loose, then gathered his belongings and slung them over his shoulders despite the dull stab of pain. He would walk until Prince healed and could handle the weight again. For a moment, sadness pierced Sean's heart at the thought of Prince never carrying anything again.

*What if Prince cannot make the journey? What will I do with him?*

But that time had not come, and perhaps Prince would recover. Sean took one last glance at the cave and smiled at the idea that the Lord had provided him shelter in such a timely fashion. As he grabbed a blueberry muffin out of his saddlebag, he closed his eyes.

"Thank You for this day and this food, Lord. Please protect Mama and Papa, and please direct my steps. Amen."

How blessed he was to have food to eat and a horse to carry him and keep him company. Pulling his scarf around his neck, he led Prince along the stream in search of Micah's grotto.

# Chapter Five

Down in the colliery, Mac made mental notes of every place where the guards herded him. From what he saw, several tunnels branched out from a central chamber and hundreds of armed soldiers guarded the tunnels, each brandishing a scimitar that glistened in the mine's torchlight. A few henchmen also prowled the colliery, and when a captive near Mac paused to catch his breath, one darted forward from the shadows and lashed several strips of oil-soaked leather across the man's exposed back. The tunnel amplified the prisoner's screams of pain as they echoed off the walls and rang in Mac's ears.

Sweat rolled down Mac's back despite the chill. His chest burned every time a guard passed him, but he knew how foolish it would be to take them on when they surrounded him. He would wait for God to show him what to do and when to do it.

"There's no hope of escaping, gentlemen," a voice boomed. Mac glanced over his shoulder at the guard who stood with his hands on his hips, his oily black hair spilling over huge shoulders. "Dragons are perched at every exit in case you decide to wander off to enjoy the fresh autumn air. And we are short on dragon food." Raucous laughter from the other guards filled the cavernous hall.

Mac used thoughts of returning to his family to motivate him as he chipped away at the mine's walls, his shoulders often bumping those of the men around him. The acrid reek of sweat and urine filled the mine. Some men fainted, and the guards tossed them to the side until they revived. Others threw down their picks and allowed the guards to drag them away.

"You are welcome to quit whenever you wish. We will escort you to Nafaar's private lair where you will meet his hungry babies."

Ravenous squawks followed the departure of the rebellious captives, along with occasional screams. A few guards returned with the men bruised and bleeding but eager to pick up their axes and swing at the wall again. Other men never returned.

Mac whispered prayers every hour, and during one prayer, he glanced over to see two colliers watching. They nodded, and the three whispered introductions over the course of the next hour. His new friends, William and Erin, sought any safe opportunity to pray with Mac in secret, and Mac encouraged them with Bible verses as often as he could.

\* \* \* \*

As Sean walked along the stream, the sound of the water rushing over the rocks soothed him. Songbirds whistled their way from one branch to another, swooping and circling Sean and Prince along the water's edge. A brown, speckled trout leaped from the stream and performed a pirouette before landing back in the water with a wet slap. Aside from the chilly winds, the forest remained pleasant, and any ice on the surface of puddles had melted.

Within a few hours, Prince's legs started to tremble. Sean considered leaving his horse to rest and graze by the stream, but he remembered the howls that had awakened him during the night. Tying up a horse here would only guarantee a pile of bones when he returned.

As images of hungry wolves ran through Sean's mind, his eyes caught a flash of white at the side of a hill about ten meters in front of them. Eyes like molten gold fixed upon them, and Sean stopped so abruptly that Prince collided with his back, knocking him forward a step. The wolf tensed then curled back its black lips to bare its long canine fangs.

A burst of adrenaline surged through Sean's veins, and his jaw dropped as the wolf crouched, its hind legs coiled. The birds stopped singing, and only the splashing stream broke the still air. Then, a low rumble. Behind Sean, Prince snorted and stepped back, then gave a shrill neigh.

As Sean stood between the wolf and his horse, he realized the wolf might decide that he was an easier target than a horse with sharp hooves. He reached for his sword, keeping his eyes on the wolf. Its growl grew louder, and as Sean drew his weapon the animal snarled and snapped its jaws. Prince snorted and whinnied and tugged on the reins. Sean clung to them and, praying for protection and guidance, raised his sword.

A snarl ripped from the wolf's throat as it bounded toward him, and as Sean lifted the sword, a voice rang out beyond the wolf.

"Stay!"

The animal drove its stiff legs down into the grass and came to a jarring halt less than a meter in front of Sean, staring up at him with yellow eyes and a rattling growl. Prince squealed and swung his head back, pulling Sean off balance. As the wolf crouched and watched the pair, a tall man stepped out from behind the hill and approached them. Sean looked up, his arm shaking from the weight of the raised sword.

The man ran a hand over his trimmed white beard, then held out his other hand. "I apologize for the scare, but Sam is territorial and quite protective of me. I am Micah."

*Micah!* Sean fumbled as he returned his sword to its sheath and extended his trembling hand. "My ... my name is Sean," he said, out of breath. His heart thudded against his ribs.

Micah shook his hand with a firm grip, then released it and stared at Sean. A pair of tiny spectacles framed his hazel eyes. After a moment, Sean pointed at Sam. "Is that a wolf?"

Micah looked down and touched the wolf's head. The growl faded. "Yes, he is. I discovered Sam as a pup foraging for food a few years ago, so I took him in." Micah eyed Prince and then studied Sean's face. "What brings you here?"

Sean's shoulders sagged, and his head spun a little. *Vicar Perry ... Papa.* He looked up at Micah. "Do you mind if I sit down?"

"As you wish, but if you prefer, my home is right over that crest," Micah said, pointing. "I have a much more comfortable seat there, as well as fish and tea I prepared this morning."

His words brought to Sean's mind the aroma of his mother's fish suppers—cooked cod or haddock splashed with malt vinegar. Or the smoked salmon and cream cheese on toasted bread his father once brought home for him. Sean's mouth watered.

"That sounds wonderful. Thank you."

Micah turned and strode around the side of the hill. The wolf darted after him, and as Sean pulled on Prince's reins, the horse, breathing hard, reluctantly followed. His nostrils flared and the whites of his eyes showed as the boy and his horse passed the spot where Sam had launched his attack.

As Sean caught up to Micah, he studied the slender man. Long gray hair hung just below Micah's shoulders, and he wore an old jacket, dirty trousers, and a pair of roughly hewn leather boots. Sean remembered Vicar Perry's words: *He's a kind man, and I believe he will give you godly direction in more ways than one.* Micah was obviously a man of few words, and he seemed almost disinterested, but Sean still sensed he could trust the man.

# Chapter Six

S et against the base of a steep hill, the portal to Micah's grotto was approximately four meters high, and three meters wide. A crystalline spring bubbled from a chasm at the foot of the cavern and spilled into the stream below where a small, arched wooden bridge provided a path to the other side.

As Micah parted the canvas covering the entranceway and Sam loped inside, Sean set down his supplies and tied Prince to a nearby tree. Then he followed Micah into a cavernous room.

"Please make yourself at home."

Micah walked over to a large, handcrafted kitchen cupboard, while Sean sat down at a small wooden table. As he looked around, he realized that the crystalline stream outside came from a large, spring-fed pool that bubbled up into the grotto from an underground aquifer deep within the hill behind them. Brightly colored trout swam in the clear pool and planters of beautiful, fragrant flowers filled the grotto. A fissure in the ceiling above the water allowed enough light to reveal multi-colored stones at the bottom of the reservoir, and iridescent reflections flashed across the pool walls. In the kitchen area where

Micah prepared dinner sat a dark, wooden desk, covered with small piles of dried plants, flowers, seeds, and twisted roots in a variety of shapes and sizes

Sean cocked his head. "What are the dried flowers and roots for?"

Micah wiped his hands with a cloth and leaned against the cupboard. "I create herbal remedies to help lessen, if not cure, illnesses. I am not a physician, of course, but I believe one of the purposes behind plants and flowers is to provide us with a means of natural healing."

Glancing at the barren table, Micah opened a cupboard door and pulled out two plates and utensils. Sean imagined his mother prodding him in the side to help. *You're a guest*, she always said. Even though his mother was not here to prod him, Sean stood and walked over to Micah, who was grinding chunks of salt into smaller particles.

"I tend to the people in Keswick when they fall ill, especially when the doctor cannot help them. I do my best not to interfere with him because he serves a good purpose too, but God has given me the ability to help people with their illnesses. I even helped a little boy who we later learned had ingested poison in his family's barn."

As Sean set the table, he glanced over at the farthest corner. In the shadows sat Micah's four-poster bed, covered with a handmade down comforter. A small nightstand with a worn leather-bound Bible and a brass oil lamp stood beside the bed. Flickering candles occupied several miniature alcoves in the walls, and the light gave the living area a dim but appealing glow. Sam's white pelt caught Sean's eye from where the wolf lay on a bright red woolen rug, which added a splash of color to the stone floor. The animal never took its eyes off him.

Sean looked along the wall toward the front. A warm blaze hissed and crackled from a large cavity carved into the stone wall, with a primitive but effective tin flue toward the back. Two copper kettles of boiling water hung from an iron brace stretched across the fireplace, as well as metal hooks with several trout. Against the wall sat a large column of firewood. Sean inhaled the crisp smell of burning wood and seared trout.

"Would you mind saying the blessing over this meal, Sean?" Micah asked. He placed two bountiful platters of trout and potatoes on the table and then sat across from Sean.

"Sure." Sean clasped his hands and bowed his head. "Lord, we thank You for the meal we are about to receive. Please allow it to nourish our bodies. I also pray Your peace and protection over this home. In the name of Jesus, amen."

"Thank you for that blessing." Micah smiled and reached for the teapot. "Let me pour your tea; it's steaming hot."

While Micah enjoyed a leisurely meal, Sean shoveled food into his mouth.

Micah gave a chuckle as he watched Sean. "I don't believe I have enough trout in the entire pool to satisfy you!"

Sean looked up, then set his fork down and chewed a piece of trout. He could not identify the blend of spices, but they mixed in his mouth with bursts of flavor. "I'm sorry. As good as my mother's cooking is, it cannot rival your trout. This is delicious."

Micah nodded with a small smile. "Well, thank you. When you eat as much fish as I do, you're always looking for new ways to prepare it." After he had eaten, Micah leaned back in his chair and sighed. "Now, what brings you up here?"

Sean swallowed his mouthful of potatoes. "Vicar Perry said you might help me."

"Ah, good old Vicar Perry, a wonderful man of God," Micah said, smiling, "He and Mrs. Perry are well, I trust?"

Sean nodded, wiping his mouth with his sleeve. He'd been trying to mind his manners, but Micah did not seem to mind his voraciousness.

"Good," Micah said. "I am glad to hear that. Now, what can I help you with?"

Sean sat up from his plate and focused on Micah. "Do you know about the kidnappings?"

Micah nodded. "Yes, or at least I have heard about them." He scooted his chair back and stretched out his legs. "I traveled to the village for supplies several days ago, and overheard a few conversations about it. No one knows many details, but I hear Lady Silver and her dragons might be involved. And then, on the night I returned home, I heard a scream."

Sean sucked in a breath. *Were those papa's screams?*

39

Micah sat up and pulled his chair closer to the table. "I stepped outside, and I know it sounds strange, but the scream came from the sky. It didn't make sense to me until I remembered the stories I had heard. Of course it was dark and cloudy, so I couldn't see anything. After a few moments, the cries trailed off, and I returned to pray beside my bed." Micah shook his head. "It was the eeriest thing. I still hear that scream if I think about it. It's hard to shake."

He paused. "I must tell you, Sean, I was not surprised to see you. I sensed a visitor coming and I asked the One who is wiser than all to prepare me so that I could help whomever needed it. Perhaps you are that visitor."

Sean's mind drifted from Micah's words as he remembered the black dragon and his father's screams.

Perhaps Micah had heard his father. Nafaar had dragged him across the sky and through the wind while his father screamed and kicked. His chest tightened and his mouth grew dry.

*All because I didn't want to close a gate.*

The full weight of his guilt fell upon Sean's heart. He dropped his head and sobbed. "They kidnapped my father."

As Sean focused on taking slow, deep breaths, Micah placed his hand on Sean's arm. "I am so sorry. What can I do to help?"

"Vicar Perry thought you could help me find Alexander."

"I am afraid Alexander may be unable to help anyone anymore." Micah shook his head, then stood and walked to the fireplace. While he stoked the flickering logs, he continued, "Dreadful news travels faster than good, and even the remote village of Keswick already heard of Evangeline's death and the fight between Alexander and Nafaar. If Alexander is even still alive, I'm afraid he may be dying of a broken heart."

"Do you know where his lair is?"

Micah returned to his seat. "I can direct you there, but he may not be able to help you."

"I have to try because if he can't help, then I will have to find my father myself."

With a small measure of dramatic flourish, Micah lowered his head and peered over the top of his spectacles at Sean. "That would not be wise. If Lady Silver is behind Evangeline's death and these kidnappings, you cannot possibly be prepared to face someone so ruthless. She has tried to overthrow the king for years, and so far— because of Alexander's help, I might add—she has failed."

"I have no choice. I can't just sit at home and wait to see who … who gets the power. I have to go. I am supposed to go. And I want to find the dragon that kidnapped my father and I want him dead!" Sean slammed his fist down on the table, making the plates rattle.

"You will have a difficult time finding out which dragon kidnapped your father, Sean. They all look similar, and Alexander killed Nafaar, the only dragon with a silver spur on his—"

"The dragon that kidnapped my father had a silver spur on his forehead!"

41

Micah stared at Sean for a moment and then said in a low voice, "Are you certain?"

"Yes."

"Then Alexander did not finish this." Micah sighed, his eyes drifting to the fireplace. "And he more than likely does not know Nafaar is still alive."

Heavy silence passed between them before Micah spoke again. "I do not believe it would be a good idea to even consider facing Lady Silver and her dragons without help. If you cannot get Alexander to help, then it would be better to let the king handle this. I'm sure he is working on—"

"I'm sure he is, Micah, but I still have to go. I can't go home without trying."

# Chapter Seven

"I see my powers of persuasion have fallen short in trying to get you to turn around and go home. But at least I can give you a map." Micah smiled. "It will show you the location of Alexander's lair, and I just might have a few other items that will help you. I will pray for you every day. I just hope your journey doesn't take you across Lady Silver's path."

"Do you think Alexander is still alive?"

Micah shrugged, then pushed his chair back and stood. "I hope so. If he is not and Nafaar is, then it will take more than your courage and the king's forces to overpower Lady Silver and her dragons. Now let's get a map for you."

Walking over to the nightstand, Micah opened a drawer and retrieved a sheet of parchment, a feather, and a small bottle of ink. He settled back down at the dining table, dipped the stem of the feather into the ink, and drew a simple map.

"Travel due south from here to the southernmost peaks of the Cumbrian Mountain range. It shouldn't take more than a day or so to reach by horse—"

"I have to walk," Sean interjected. "I doubt Prince can travel any farther. In fact, would you mind if I let him stay here with you? He won't be any trouble."

"Of course he can stay. But I must tell you, this journey is not meant for the soles of your shoes to bear. You will require a horse, and a strong one at that."

Nails clicked against the stone as Sam padded over to lie down on the floor next to Micah. Glancing down at his plate, Micah picked up his leftover fish and dropped it in front of Sam, who snapped it off the floor and gulped it down. Micah laid down the feathered quill.

"This map will get you to Alexander's lair. Just look for the tallest mountain surrounded by a ring of smaller mountains, and you will find his lair on the south face."

Sean studied the map. "Alexander doesn't know me. How will he respond?"

"As a sign of peace and good will, approach him with a gift of food. You will cross a stream at the base of his mountain, so take the time to catch a stringer of fish. When you arrive near the entrance, do not enter his lair. Lay down the fish and state that I sent you. Hopefully, he will come to you."

"Will he understand what I say?"

"Dragons have a high level of intelligence and have coexisted with us for centuries, albeit from a distance. Many that come into close contact with us, like Alexander and Nafaar, have learned the meanings of many words and phrases. But I must tell you, Sean,

44

Alexander may not be as strong as he was before Evangeline died. I will pray he helps you, and all of England for that matter." Micah rose and walked to the fireplace to fetch more hot tea.

"How far is Lady Silver's castle from Alexander's lair?" Sean asked.

Glancing at Sean, Micah hesitated. "Perhaps two or three days' ride to the far north of the Cumbrian Mountains." Micah refilled Sean's cup. "It's hard to say; I've never made the journey."

"God knows how long this trip to Alexander's lair will take without Prince," Sean said.

Micah patted him on the shoulder. "You can take my horse, Paladin. He's only three years old and has three times the energy I have ever seen in a stallion."

Sean stared up at Micah with wide eyes. "Are you sure? You will have no means to travel!"

"Of course I'm sure. I believe we are seeing God's plan unfold, don't you think?"

Sean smiled and nodded.

"Oh, one moment." Micah strode to his bed and kneeled, then pulled out a handmade wooden chest and opened it. Sifting through the items inside, he pulled out a long animal horn on a leather strap. As Micah handed it to Sean, the flickering firelight threw shadows across the Hebrew script engraved along the horn's shaft.

"This is a Hebrew *shofar*—something like a trumpet. My great-grandfather passed it on to me when I was about your age. He fashioned it out of a ram's horn over a hundred years ago when he served as a trusted advisor to the king. According to him, it can summon Alexander; the wind carries its notes for great distances. He prayed that only a righteous man's breath would give it sound, lest Alexander be summoned for evil."

Micah smiled at Sean. "Alexander learned to recognize it as a call for help. I should have given it to the king, but there has never been any occasion to use it until now. I want you to take it on your journey. It may come in handy."

Sean traced the smooth horn and the edges of the engravings with one finger. "But Micah, this must mean so much to you."

"Indeed, it does. But I believe it will be of more use to you than me, and I know you will take good care of it."

"I will, I promise. Thank you. I will return it to you safe and sound." Sean held it up and studied the script. "What does it say?"

"It is taken from Psalm 59: Deliver me from my enemies, O God; protect me from those who rise up against me. Deliver me from evildoers, and save me from bloodthirsty men."

Sean cradled it as Micah walked back to the fireplace and asked, "Did you eat enough to hold you for a little while?"

"Yes, thank you." Sean plucked the last morsel of fish from his plate and popped it into his mouth, savoring its tang.

"Let us go down to the stable now," Micah said. "I will introduce you to Paladin."

As they walked out of the grotto, they passed Prince, whose attention had drifted from fear to boredom and now grazed a few meters from the tree. As Sam loped past him, Prince snorted and jumped away, then stood at the end of his rope stamping his hooves.

Sean and Micah followed Sam along the path parallel to the stream until they came upon a simple wooden structure near the water's edge. A full bin of wheat and straw sat against the stable, and the surrounding trees provided plenty of shade.

Micah kicked a pebble from the path. "Paladin spends most of his time here, except during the spring when the rain floods the stream."

As they approached, Micah whistled. Hooves pounded up the bank as a massive black horse galloped up to greet Micah. As he neared, powerful muscles shifted under his glossy coat, and a blaze of white ran from his ears to his nostrils. Sean stared.

Micah hugged Paladin's neck, then removed his spectacles and wiped them clean. "Because of the wolves in this part of England, I find it unwise to tether Paladin. Instead of restricting his mobility, I let him live unfettered by any constraints. His immense strength would make any predator, including a wolf, unwise to confront him."

Sam loped in a wide circle around Paladin, and the horse turned with perked ears toward the wolf. "How do Sam and Paladin get along?" Sean asked.

"Sam is the only wolf Paladin considers a friend. I raised them together, so Sam considers Paladin a pack mate and would face a pack of wolves to protect Paladin."

Sam dropped into a play bow and then sprang away when the massive horse whinnied and charged him. Paladin's hooves hammered the ground, and Sean felt the powerful vibrations beneath his feet.

"I can't believe you're lending him to me," Sean said.

"I'm not," Micah said. Sean glanced at Micah, who smiled. "I'm giving him to you. I feel God would want me to do this, so receive it as though from Him."

Sean stared at Micah, his mouth open. "No, I can't."

"You must. You will never reach Alexander's lair without Paladin to get you there."

"I don't know what to say," Sean said. He approached the black horse, then reached for him. As he ran his hand through the coarse mane, Paladin pressed his flat, velvety nose against Sean's chest, breathed in, expelled a loud breath, and turned away.

Turning back to Micah, Sean grinned. "Thank you so much! Are you sure? If I could just borrow him—"

"No, no, you must have him for your own. I am old and cannot care for him as well as a younger person."

The giddiness that rose in Sean's chest took his breath away and filled his eyes with tears. "Thank you, Micah. And … please keep Prince for yourself. He will heal well, I'm sure."

"It's a deal!" Micah smiled. "Thank you, Sean. I will take good care of him."

Sean watched Paladin chase Sam until Micah turned back to him. "Now that I have introduced you to Paladin, why don't we enjoy one more cup of tea before bed? You will need a good night's rest before you begin your journey."

The sun still shone beyond the forest's canopy, but the blue sky was growing darker with each minute. The horizon already glowed yellow with a hint of orange. Sean nodded. "Again, thank you. Do you think I might have a few more bites of fish too?"

"Of course!"

As they walked back, Sam streaked past them with his ears perked and his jaws wide, almost as though he were grinning. *Perhaps wolves have a lighter side after all.* Sean and Micah followed Sam to the grotto and spent the evening in front of the fire—drinking, eating, and speculating about the future.

# Chapter Eight

Deep in Lady Silver's mine, another grueling day of forced labor came to a close as the guards allowed the captives to retire for the night. Beyond one tunnel entrance, the scarlet sun slipped below the horizon. The guards passed out bowls of lukewarm porridge to the men, and as Mac and Erin ate, William left his porridge untouched and reclined against the stone wall. When Erin collapsed into a deep sleep, Mac draped a blanket over his friend before returning to William.

For the last day or two, William had only spoken when asked a question. His brown hair matted to his forehead, he now clenched his jaw and kept his eyes on the silhouette of the dragon perched at the tunnel's entrance. William's bouts of delirium were increasing, but there were moments when his mind cleared. It was then when he watched the changing of the guards.

As Mac leaned back against the wall, William turned to him, his eyes bloodshot. "I heard the guards talking about a river down below where they get fish to feed the dragons every morning. I'm going to jump."

"Forget it, William. You'll never survive the fall," Mac whispered.

William shot furtive glances in every direction and then turned back to Mac. "I have no choice. I can't stay here for one more day."

Mac leaned close. "What's your plan?"

"When the dragons change guards, they leave this opening unattended for about twelve seconds. I'll make a run for it and jump into the river. Then I can go find help."

"What if the river is too shallow?"

William lowered his head. "I just don't have your strength, Mac. I can't take another day of this. I would rather face a hungry dragon."

"I can't talk you out of this?"

William shook his head.

Mac placed his hand on his friend's shoulder. "You just might be the bravest man in here, William. I don't think I could make that leap."

"You could if you were as desperate as I am."

"Well, it would be wonderful if you could get word to the king. But before you charge into the night, let me pray with you."

Both men scanned the area and then bowed their heads.

"Father, we are in a desperate situation. I am struggling with William's decision, but he has made up his mind. Please help him and rescue us from this danger. In Jesus' name we pray. Amen."

They shared a brief hug and lay down on their makeshift blankets on the cold stone floor. Within a few minutes, Mac drifted into a

51

restless sleep, but he awoke later to the scraping of William's feet. Looking up with bleary eyes, he saw William bolt down the tunnel. The moonlight flickered off his friend's hair as William leaped out of the tunnel's entrance and headlong into the night.

Mac's heart raced. He almost had to cling to the ground to stop himself from jumping up and running after William. As he lay curled against the wall, curses echoed down the tunnel and heavy boots pounded past him. Then a distant splash reached him, and he hid a smile as the footsteps stopped at the end of the tunnel.

"Bloody idiot. He's as good as dead anyway. Go send Nafaar. Either Nafaar will find him, or he will freeze to death."

As the cold made Mac shiver, he clung to his blanket and prayed for William.

\* \* \* \*

Free-falling toward the river below, William tried to position his body so that he would enter the river feet first, but the high speed of his descent made it impossible. William had underestimated the distance to the river. Terror crept into his heart and just as he felt himself losing consciousness he slammed into the cold water with his right shoulder. The impact tore his right arm from the shoulder socket, and it took a Herculean effort to suppress his screams of agony and pain.

He struggled to stay afloat in the icy, black water, but the strong current that was sweeping him downstream made him weaker and, without the use of his right arm, he simply did not have the strength to continue treading water and trying to swim out of the current and to the shore. But as William began to recite the Lord's Prayer, his good hand grabbed hold of a tree branch that was partially submerged. The pale, silky light of a three-quarter moon revealed that the branch was attached to a great oak, felled by lightning and stretched halfway across the river. Using what little strength he had left, William managed to climb onto a stronger neighboring branch that enabled him to climb out of the water.

In spite of the searing pain in his shoulder and the bitter cold of the water, William was grateful to have a secure branch above the water where he could rest. Dangerous as it might be, he knew that the river was still the fastest mode of transportation to avoid detection by the dragon sentries.

*Just a little farther. As much as it hurts, I must move quickly before the guards discover I'm gone and send the dragons into the sky to search for me.*

As William scanned the river bank near him he saw a thick branch of the fallen oak bobbing loosely in the water just a few meters away. William had hoped for better than this. He knew that he owed it to Mac and Erin to give it his best shot. With all of his might he lifted himself onto the old oak branch, pushed away from the tree, and floated downstream. He was trying not to care about the pain and cold because now, at least, he was free.

After a few minutes, the river began to narrow and William noticed an increase in the number of tall, willowy trees that lined both sides of the river. Most of the leaves had surrendered to the autumn winds, but the arching branches still provided an occasional canopy.

*Thank God. These trees will provide me some cover.*

As William continued to float through this botanical tunnel, he glimpsed a swift and fleeting shadow pass above him. Now the fear returned with a fury. William was unable to stall his progress as the current swept him toward a vulnerable stretch of open sky.

*No! No! No! I'll be fair game!*

But as he floated out into the open again, he could not see any dragons waiting for him. He looked all around him, but it seemed the threat had passed. William let out a sigh of relief and continued downriver looking for a place of refuge from the frigid water and the dragons who might be still stalking him. But as soon as hope rose in his heart, terror struck it down.

The current suddenly surged and William was unable to fight it. He saw another fallen tree up ahead, but what he saw on top of that tree made his heart sink. Raising its huge black wings, the dragon shifted its weight forward and drew back its silver talons and waited.

William knew there was nothing left to do. The distance between him and the dragon was closing too quickly. At the moment the dragon attacked, William mercifully lost consciousness. At first there was darkness, and then there was light.

# Chapter Nine

When Sean awoke the next morning on a warm pallet in front of the fireplace, Micah stood in the kitchen preparing fresh bread and assorted dried fruits. A pot of tea brewed over a low fire, and a wraith-like mist hovered above the pool, where Sean knelt and splashed icy water onto his face, the cold shocking him wide awake. As he gathered his belongings, Micah crouched in front of the fireplace and waved his hands over the fire.

"I will pray you find your father soon," Micah said, glancing at Sean and standing.

"Thank you, Micah."

"I took the liberty of placing a pair of woolen gloves in your knapsack. I noticed you weren't wearing any yesterday."

"Vicar Perry was right," Sean said. "You helped me more than I could have imagined."

Micah smiled. "Your faith and obedience drew this favor, and they will see you through your journey."

When Sean and Micah finished breakfast, they bundled up and walked to Paladin's stable as Sam ran ahead. Neither spoke, preferring instead to enjoy the soothing rustle of leaves tumbling across the grass. Sadness tugged at Sean's heart; he would miss Micah.

As they approached the stable, Paladin emerged and trotted towards the pair.

"Good boy, good boy," Micah said, petting the horse's nose. He retrieved a simple leather saddle off the stable wall and hoisted it up onto Paladin's back, pulling the cinch just snug enough to avoid chafing while still providing a safe ride for Sean. Then he placed a metal bit into Paladin's mouth and pulled the reins over the horse's neck.

After Micah stepped away, Sean secured his belongings to the saddle and mounted Paladin. The horse shifted beneath him and twisted his ears back to listen to Sean adjust his sword for the ride and place the shofar's leather strap around his neck. Sean patted Paladin, and the horse glanced back at him with shining eyes.

"Micah, I feel like I was born to ride this horse."

Micah nodded, folding his arms. "I took him to the village blacksmith for new shoes a month ago, so he should be fine for the journey."

"I'll never forget you, Micah." Sean reached down to shake his hand. "Thank you again."

"Go in God's peace, Sean. I will keep you in my prayers."

Sam approached Micah and then stared up at Sean and Paladin. Despite the white wolf's aloofness toward him, Sean felt a pang of pity. Sam was losing his friend, and Micah would replace Paladin with old Prince who would never play with a wolf. But Micah could give Prince a more comfortable life than the old horse would receive on the farm.

Sean nudged Paladin, and as the horse broke into a spry canter down the path, Sean looked over his shoulder and waved to Micah.

* * * *

When the guards awoke the captives that morning, the two guards who handed Mac and Erin their porridge sneered at each other.

"Did you hear about the idiot who tried to escape?"

Mac almost dropped the porridge, but kept his head down and his eyes on the dish.

The other guard chuckled. "I hear Nafaar didn't come back for a while, but when he did, he wasn't hungry anymore."

Erin's spoon fell against the bowl with a loud clank. As the guards moved down the row of men, Mac's gray porridge blurred as hot tears cut through the grime on his cheeks. Pain cut into his chest and silent sobs wracked his shoulders, but he forced a spoonful into his mouth.

Later that day, Erin studied Mac. "We can't give up now. We can't lose hope."

"I don't know what to think anymore, Erin. It looks hopeless."

"I know. It does look hopeless, but we have to trust God. We can't lose hope."

Erin helped Mac to his feet and prayed for him as the guards prowled the halls, screaming for the men to come alive and get back to work. As the other captives took their positions, it took all Mac had to lift his mining pick.

He thought of Cynthia and Sean, and the healing began.

\* \* \* \*

Up to this point in his journey, Sean had enjoyed a relatively clear path along the stream. But now the landscape was dotted with ancient gnarled oaks whose roots twisted here and there among large stones strewn along the way. When Paladin began stumbling over the roots and rocks, Sean dismounted and walked ahead until he found clearer ground. As the terrain rose towards a hill to the southwest, Sean left the familiar stream and climbed. He wanted to find easier footing and a high point where he could see the lay of the land.

As Sean and Paladin clambered up the large hill, the trees thinned and the boy and his horse emerged into a small clearing. Cold shadows fell back as Sean and Paladin broke free of the forest's reach and stood on the crest of the hill. After navigating the dark forest for several hours, Sean had lost all sense of time and he felt a pang of desperation at the sight of the setting sun. Its rays bathed the field in a tangerine glow, and as the tops of the clouds grew darker, the setting sun flamed across their undersides and painted them orange and gold.

To the south, a majestic mountain range spread before him with a single peak rising above the others. Would he find his father in time? Would Alexander help him? Was the dragon watching from that peak at that very moment? How well could dragons see? Could Alexander see Sean?

*What if he's hungry?*

Setting his anxious thoughts aside, Sean scanned the distance he still had to travel. More than he could cover in one day.

"Do you think we can reach that mountain by tomorrow evening, Paladin?" The horse gave a soft snort and pawed the ground. Sean ran his fingertips across the horse's thick, dark mane and then grinned. "I do too!"

Off to the side of the field a large weeping willow perched on an incline near a shallow pond. Its branches created a curtain that grazed the ground and hid the trunk from view. Long, drooping branches rippled in the breeze, and Sean parted the leafy curtain with one hand to duck inside. The sunset's glow still touched the tree's furrowed gray bark, but the thick branches hid him from the outside world.

Paladin nickered and stamped his hoof on the other side of the curtain, so Sean slipped out and led the horse inside the tree's shelter. Paladin lowered himself to rest in the soft grass while Sean pulled off his boots and laid his sword beside him. Then, curling up against the tree's cradling roots, Sean wrapped himself in his blanket and laid his head on his lumpy knapsack.

As soon as he fell asleep, nightmares about Nafaar flying away with his father woke him. He dozed off again after his heart slowed back down, but the nightmares broke his sleep several times throughout the night. He prayed for relief, and even as waves of fatigue swept over him, he fought against sleep lest he face the nightmares again and again. Finally, he fell into a restless slumber for the remainder of the night.

# Chapter Ten

A t dawn, the sunlight did not touch the tree's shade, and even the gentle rain did not rouse Sean. It pattered on the ground beyond the tree but did not reach the tree's trunk where Paladin and Sean slept. But as it grew louder and pounded against the ground, a great roar woke Sean.

Springing up, Sean pulled his sword from its sheath. As Paladin rolled to his hooves and snorted, another mighty roar shook the willow's leaves. Sean strode past Paladin and cautiously stepped through the curtain of leaves into the pouring rain. No more than a hundred meters down the southwest side of the hill, two dragons snarled and hissed as they faced each other, one half the size of the other.

On the perimeter, a young boy squinted through the rain aiming his crossbow, and shooting arrows at the larger dragon, but the arrows bounced off its olive green scales. The boy's face glistened, either from rain or tears.

Sean raced down the hillside, whipping through the cold, wet grass as icy rain stung his face. He ducked under the swooping wing of the green dragon, almost sliding in the mud, and lifted his sword.

But he hesitated. His legs shook. Would a wayward claw nick him in the stomach? Would one dragon's sudden movement knock him over or crush him?

The green dragon's underside swung above him. A forearm the size of a small tree crashed down near him, shaking the ground.

*Go!*

Sean darted forward around the dragon's side and came eye level with the glistening scales on its chest, each one the size of Sean's hand. Catching the motion out of the corner of its eye, the dragon fixed its red eyes on Sean, then drew its lips back and snarled. It pulled back one foot like a swatting cat—except this swat could fracture Sean's skull or break his neck.

Driving his heels into the ground, Sean thrust his sword into the dragon's chest. The blade struck the large scales, and then slid with a shriek to plunge into the flesh beneath them. Sean shoved the blade as deep into the dragon's chest as he could, and then withdrew it.

The dragon gave a screech that made Sean's ears ring, then staggered backward. Dark blood flowed down its slick scales as the dragon hissed and staggered backward into the forest. Sean thought better than to follow it into the shadows.

Spinning around to face the remaining dragon, Sean discovered it to be about the same size as Paladin. It crouched several meters away, the muted sunlight glinting off light grey scales rimmed with black. As the boy standing off to the side ran up the hill toward Sean, the dragon stepped back and watched Sean with luminous blue eyes. The boy came panting up to Sean, the ground squishing under his stride. Then he dropped to one knee.

"I owe you my life, sir. Thank you."

Sean took his eyes off the dragon to stare down at the blonde-headed boy, who appeared to be around fourteen years old. Sean wiped the rain out of his eyes and took a deep breath.

"Oh, stand up. I only need a handshake and an introduction. What is your name?"

The boy stood and ran both hands through his wet hair, pulling it back out of his eyes. Then he peered up at Sean. "I'm Andrew Brandt, sir. My friends call me Andy."

With disheveled hair, brown eyes, and threadbare clothes, Andy resembled a pauper looking for his next meal.

"I'm Sean Delbridge."

The rain lightened to a drizzle. Andy rested both hands on his hips as he surveyed the mountains in the distance, and then looked back at Sean.

"I am indebted to you, sir."

Sean smiled. "I appreciate your gratitude, but it's not necessary. If you would like, you can help me prepare some breakfast."

Andy shook his head. "I would rather remain in your debt until I can provide full recompense."

"Do you always talk this way?" Sean asked.

"Sir?"

"You don't have to call me 'sir.' By the looks of you, I'm only a couple of years older than you are."

Andy shrugged. "If you insist. But I still want to pay you back for your kindness and courage."

"I won't win this argument, will I?"

The boy shook his head. "No sir, you will not."

"What do your parents have to say about your being away from home?" Sean asked.

Andy looked down. "Both my parents died during the influenza outbreak when I was a lad. I ended up in an orphanage, but I ran away and have been on my own ever since. Or, I should say, Saber and I—"

His eyes widened and then he spun around and ran across the wet grass to the young serpent that now rested against a boulder. Andy scanned the animal's body and stopped to inspect a gash on its shoulder. Then he ran his hand over the dragon's muzzle as if petting a horse.

Sean watched from several meters away. "I have never been this close to a dragon before. Does it breathe fire yet?"

Andy shook his head as he spread one enormous wing and ran his hand over its membrane. If fully extended, the wing could have wrapped around Andy and cradled him.

"Saber is only eighteen months old. He hasn't learned that yet." Andy patted his companion's forehead. "That was a nasty clash, old friend, but you showed that serpent a real fight, didn't you?"

Saber looked young, but he possessed extraordinarily long wings and strong forelegs. As Andy sat on the boulder beside Saber, the dragon turned and nosed his chin, making him giggle. Sean stared at the pair. He had heard tales of people raising dragons, but he had never met one. He approached the pair.

"Will he mind if I touch him?"

Andy stroked Saber's long neck. "No, not at all. He is very gentle."

Sean reached down, and the dragon extended his neck to sniff at his outstretched fingers. Saber watched Sean as he stroked the smooth, scaly neck. After a few seconds, the dragon closed his eyes and emitted a low, guttural purr. Sean looked up at Andy.

"Is it difficult to stay on his back when flying?"

"No. My old saddle seat is not the most comfortable in the world, but the straps fasten around my waist and legs, and the stirrups help me hang on tight. Want to take him for a test flight? I can get him to do a somersault for you."

Sean imagined the ground dropping away from under him, and then him spinning as Saber somersaulted. His stomach turned, and he held up his hands. "Oh no! No offense, but you will *never* get me on a dragon."

Andy shrugged.

"Where did he come from?" Sean asked

Andy folded his arms. "I worked for a traveling festival the summer before last. I fed the animals, including Saber and a much older dragon that died. The festival owner drank all his profits and had to close down. He owed many of his workers quite a bit of back pay, but he ran off in the middle of the night, and we never heard from him again. I had grown very fond of Saber and claimed him before anyone else could. We've been together ever since."

"That's amazing. Now, can you tell me what happened earlier? Why did that dragon attack Saber?"

"He didn't at first. We had just landed to take cover from the rain and rest his wings. Saber hasn't flown for very long, you see. Then the dragon came out of the forest and charged up the hill at me, but Saber got between us."

Sean glanced toward the forest where the injured dragon had fled. At the edge of the trees, a ruby trail gleamed in the grass. Sean couldn't see far into the forest, but the bloody trail turned from a few drops into a steady line. He looked back to Andy.

"Do you think it's dead?"

Andy shrugged. As he stood, Saber slid off the boulder and trotted toward the forest, then paused and stared into the shadows like a dog listening for a deer. After a few seconds, the dragon looked over his shoulder at the boys.

"Should we find out?" Sean asked.

"What if it didn't die? It might attack us."

Saber strode forward to the edge of the forest and swept his muzzle close to the ground, nostrils flaring. He inhaled the scent of the other dragon's blood trail, then curled his lips and growled.

"Maybe Saber will keep the other dragon away," Sean said. "Besides, it's already hurt. It probably won't risk attacking us if we stay far enough away from it."

With a nod, Andy wrapped his arms around himself and descended toward Saber. Sean followed, then stopped. *Paladin.* He couldn't leave his horse tied to the willow. An injured dragon could take advantage of an easy meal like that.

"I have to get my horse first. I will meet you down there."

Sean ran back to the willow. When he ducked under the branches, Paladin stamped his feet. Sean untied the horse and guided him down the hill. As they passed the spot where the dragons had fought, Paladin snorted and tossed his head against his bit.

As they neared Andy, Saber stepped out from the shadows to face the approaching pair. Paladin drove his hooves into the ground and neighed.

"Whoa, settle down, Paladin!"

But the black horse backed away, jerking against his reins. Sean tightened his grip and shoved his palm under Paladin's whiskered nose.

"See, I've already petted the dragon. He's safe."

Paladin's hot breath touched Sean's palm, but the horse swung his head away. Sean sighed and looked back at Andy, then clung to the reins as he walked down the hill. Paladin planted his hooves into the ground.

"Come on, Paladin!" Sean tugged, but the horse tossed his head against Sean's grip. Scoffing, Sean tossed the reins down. "Fine! Stay here alone. I'm going with them."

Sean walked down to Andy. Saber stared at the horse, then turned and loped into the forest, the boys following. When Sean glanced over his shoulder, Paladin shook his mane against the misty rain, then dropped his head and followed Sean at a distance.

# Chapter Eleven

Within a few minutes of penetrating the forest, Saber bounded forward. He whisked his head close to the ground, then hopped over a few large roots and disappeared over the top of a hill. Shivering, Sean gripped the hilt of his sword and followed. Behind him, Paladin took the time to find his footing and step over the roots.

As Sean and Andy approached the crest of the hill, a volley of loud snarls and bellows exploded from the other side. The boys ran up the hill in time to see Saber barrel down it, his teeth bared and wings spread. In the small valley huddled the massive green dragon, blood pooling beneath its chest. It growled at Saber and, when the smaller dragon dashed toward its exposed hindquarters, lunged at him and drove him back. Lashing its tail, it hissed at Saber while the latter circled it.

Sean stared at the gravely wounded dragon. Even though it crouched in an effort to protect itself, it towered as tall as an elephant. Its growl was deep as it watched Saber sprint up the hill toward the boys.

Andy's gaping mouth widened into a grin. "Good job, old friend!"

He and Sean clambered down the hill, almost tripping over the roots and stones. As they approached the dragon, it swung its bulky head toward them and roared. Sean clapped his hands over his ears, but as the dragon shifted, a gleam caught his eye.

*Silver-plated talons.*

Sean gasped and turned to Andy. "This one is quite a catch."

"What do you mean?"

Sean's skin flushed, driving away the chill of the shadows. He studied the dragon as it struggled to sit up.

"This dragon belongs to Lady Silver." Then he looked up at the sky and frowned.

"I've heard of her." Andy cocked his head. "Why do you look so worried?"

"He might have reinforcements that are looking for him as we speak." Sean glanced at the blood-drenched ground beneath the serpent. "He's losing blood fast, so it's only a matter of time before he dies. We'll need to cover him with brush so they can't see him."

The pair stared at the dragon. It sank down against the earth, the forest's mottled shadows falling across its scales.

Sean took his sword in both hands and crept toward the dragon. As he neared, it turned to glare at him, and Sean froze. The dragon's breathing came in slower, shallower pants with each moment. The metallic reek of its blood filled the air as the crimson pool expanded beneath it, and the draining rainwater carried away a red stream. Sean lowered his sword.

"What are you waiting for?" Andy whispered. Sean held up his hand.

Over the next few seconds, the dragon slumped onto its side, and its head sank to the wet soil. It stared at Sean, a quiet rumble still emanating from its chest. But after a few minutes, the rumble faded, and then so did its breathing. Its glassy eyes stared out into space.

Sean sighed and put his sword back into his sheath, then walked to a bush and tore off several long branches. Andy joined him, and they tossed the branches onto the large reptile while Saber inspected every inch of the corpse. After the boys threw one last bundle onto the dragon, Sean turned to Andy.

"Once Lady Silver finds out this one is missing, other dragons will come search for him. We need to stay out of sight."

Andy glanced at the corpse covered in branches. "I wonder if we can cook it."

Sean rolled his eyes and shook his head. "The other dragons would see the smoke. But we can at least dry off. Let's go up to where I camped and eat some *real* breakfast. I will explain everything."

They climbed the hill. Paladin stood quivering at the top, and Sean patted the horse's neck. As Saber followed Andy, he glanced up at the horse before passing by. Though Paladin shied away, the horse perked his ears and turned to watch the dragon.

Sean tugged on the reins, and this time Paladin followed.

# Chapter Twelve

S ean and Andy sat near the willow tree and ate some of the bread and fruit spread Micah had provided. In the field nearby, Paladin grazed while Saber gulped down the last of the salted kippers. After both boys wrapped themselves in blankets, Sean told Andy about his father's kidnapping, his time with Micah, and his own quest to find Alexander. Andy listened with wide eyes as he placed the last morsel of food into his mouth.

"What will you do?"

"I have to find Alexander to see if he can help. If he can't, I'll find a way to help my father myself."

"I wish you the best, Sean, and thank you for the food."

"You are welcome," Sean replied, cupping his hands over his mouth and then exhaling to warm them. "Perhaps one day you can meet Micah and enjoy his cooking too."

Andy poured water from a pouch over his hands, then shook them off. "It sounds like you and Micah have been friends for a long time."

Sean smiled as he looked out over the English countryside. "Yes, it does seem like we have known each other for ages. Next to my father and Vicar Perry, he is the wisest and most God-fearing man I have ever met."

Andy rose and walked over to Saber, turning his back to Sean.

"Are you all right, Andy?"

Andy knelt beside Saber. "I was once a Christian. My parents were devoted believers, and my father feared God too." Andy patted Saber's forehead, then sat next to the dragon and draped his arm across Saber's long neck. Saber rested his head on Andy's lap.

"I'm sorry you lost your parents," Sean said. "You aren't a believer any more?"

"It wasn't fair that they died so early," Andy replied, scowling. "I needed them. How could a loving God allow that?"

Sean prayed for wisdom. "I know it can be hard to understand, Andy, but God did not *take* them from you. One of life's greatest mysteries is why God allows certain things to happen. As Christians, our faith in God helps us get through hard times with the hope that if we endure, we will overcome and see our loved ones again in Heaven. One of my favorite verses in the Bible is: *And we know that in all things God works for the good of those who love Him, who have been called according to His purpose."*

"Well, I guess I just don't have enough faith left to be a Christian," Andy whispered.

Sean's heart ached over the boy's sadness. "Andy, where will you go from here?"

Andy shrugged. "I have no place to go because I have no home. My parents were my only family, and my only friends are Saber and my books." He untied a weighty leather satchel from the back of his saddle and opened it.

Sean peered inside at the heap of well-worn books. His jaw dropped. "Have you read all those?"

Andy nodded. "Some I've read two or three times." He stroked Saber, who closed his eyes and made a humming, purring sound of pure contentment.

"Where did you learn to read?"

"They taught me the basics at the orphanage, and then I learned the rest on my own. I'm going to be a writer!"

Sean smiled. "I have an idea. Why don't you come with me? We will search for Alexander, and together we will see what God does."

"I'm just a kid. What use could I be?"

"David was just a kid when he defeated Goliath."

Andy shook his head. "I can't help you face this Lady Silver and her dragon."

"I saw you face that dragon earlier. You have great courage!" Sean studied Andy's face. "Look, I would enjoy your company. What do you say?"

Andy jumped to his feet—waking Saber—and grinned. "Well, I guess I do owe you my life, and I did promise to return the good deed." He slapped his thigh. "All right then, but Saber goes everywhere I go. Agreed?"

"Agreed!"

Both boys beamed as they shook hands.

"Do you see that tallest mountain?" Sean pointed. "That's where Alexander lives. We must hurry if we're to reach it before the sun sets."

"We have to walk? Saber and I don't walk much anymore."

"Sorry, Andy, but unless you have a better idea …"

"Perhaps Saber could fly us—"

"I said `a *better* idea!'"

"All right, all right," Andy said. "How do you know Alexander is even alive?"

Sean looked toward the mountains. "He has to be."

"What are we waiting for then? Let's go!"

After preparing Paladin for the rest of the day's journey, Sean mounted the horse and then extended his hand to hoist Andy up to sit behind him. The grass glistened as Paladin trotted down the hill. Alongside the horse, Saber loped in his awkward dragon fashion.

# Chapter Thirteen

At the mine, another grueling day of labor resumed, and with thoughts of his family and trust in God, Mac's hope for freedom grew again. His affection for Erin also deepened; Erin's prayer and encouraging whispers helped renew Mac's spirits. And although Mac had grown thinner due to the meager diet, his lean and muscular frame had taken on even more definition.

Whenever Mac felt a tug of sadness, he looked for something or someone to appreciate. If any blessing could be found in this nightmare, it would be the growing number of men who were turning their hearts and lives over to God. He and Erin encouraged the other colliers whenever the opportunity arose to hold onto hope that God would deliver them all from this evil.

Many men turned their lives over to Christ, but many refused, and they belittled those who talked about their faith that God would intervene on their behalf—especially George Disbrow. While Disbrow avoided confrontations with Mac, he enjoyed insulting Erin, who ignored him. Erin didn't have much choice.

On one occasion when Erin was praying for Disbrow, the latter shoved Erin from behind. A hulking figure of a man, Disbrow towered over Erin, his short black hair contrasting against his bushy beard. His thick eyebrows were nearly grown together across the bridge of his beak-like nose.

"I'm so sorry, friend." Disbrow spread his arms. "Me clumsy feet always get in the way. Won't you pray for me?"

A few men chuckled. Mac had heard the same men whispering among themselves, asking how any dragon could seize a mighty man like Disbrow. One captive said it took two dragons. The guards allowed Disbrow to work just enough to avoid a lashing.

Erin stood and turned to Disbrow, his blue eyes glinting in the torchlight. But before Erin could answer, Mac lay down his mining pick and stepped up to Disbrow until they almost touched noses. "What's your problem, mate?"

Disbrow winced but didn't move. "I'm not your mate, and I don't have a problem. Why don't you mind your own business?"

Several guards hovered at the periphery, their glazed eyes now bright and fixed on the two men. A good row would break the morning's monotony.

"Looking out for my friends is my business." Mac folded his arms across his chest. "If you had any brains, you would consider yourself my friend as well. It would be better if we all stuck together. Don't you agree?"

A few men inched forward to get a closer look.

Disbrow's eyebrows shot up. Then he glanced at the men around them and back to Mac. "This is not the place. We'll save this for another day."

Turning around, he shoved aside several men as he returned to his station—including a guard. The guard lost his footing and fell against the wall, hitting his shoulder. As much as the guards avoided conflict with Disbrow, they could not allow a captive to lay a finger on one of their own. Three guards threw Disbrow against the wall, and two more tethered his massive arms behind his back. As all five guards held him face down on the ground, a sixth lashed him across the back with a whip.

Mac only hesitated for a moment. Then he ran forward and grabbed the wrist of the guard's whip-wielding hand in mid-air before it could strike another blow. Mac slammed his other fist into the guard's jaw with a meaty crack, sending the man to the ground. He turned to the five guards holding down Disbrow, and as he pulled a guard off, the crowd of captives sprang forward.

The sounds and word of the revolt swept through the mine. Within minutes, two dozen other guards rushed in brandishing scimitars and whips. They threw several captives against the wall, and the crowd quieted as men backed against the wall and avoided eye contact. Several clenched their jaws and shook, while others barely suppressed their grins. The guards helped up their injured partners, who identified the men who assaulted them—including Mac and Disbrow. Although Erin had jumped in to help Mac, the watchmen overlooked him.

The guards seized the rest of the men. Mac gritted his teeth as the whip tore across his back like a bolt of lightning, then came around again and ripped across the raw flesh beneath. Mac clenched his throat against a scream, even as tears streamed down his face and his nose ran. He refused to give the guards the satisfaction of hearing his pain.

After the lashing, the guards allowed the men to return to their stations. Mac stared at the bleeding welts and gashes on the backs of the men before him; his own back felt as though the guards had dipped their whips in wasp venom. But as he turned to join the other men, two guards seized him as several others grabbed Disbrow. The guards hauled their captives down the tunnel while another shouted to the captives behind them.

"One more time, and we will memorialize your names on the dragons' dinner menu."

The guards hauled Mac and Disbrow into another branch of the colliery and threw them into a dim cell with metal bars. Bones lay scattered on the cell floor, including three human skulls. Mac stared. *Strategically placed to frighten rebels like us, perhaps?* If so, it worked.

To avoid disturbing the remains of the men who had gone before them, Mac picked up every skull and bone and laid them in the center of the cell. Stepping back, he prayed silently and hoped they had gone to a better place.

Disbrow watched Mac with a smirk.

"Very nice, mate. Now, can you help me with this fetter?"

Mac motioned toward him. "Turn around."

Disbrow complied and then turned his head towards Mac with a puzzled expression. "Why did you help me?"

Mac grunted as he pulled on the restraints. "First, I care about every person God created. Second, when we became this crazy woman's captives, you and I became brothers." Mac removed the leather strap from Disbrow's wrists and tossed it to the floor.

Disbrow flexed his wrists. Then, he walked to the corner and, with plenty of grunting, lowered his prodigious frame into a corner. Mac settled into the opposite corner and gazed through the bars of the cell, inhaling the bone pile's faint scent of decay.

"Doesn't look good, does it, Delbridge?" Disbrow sighed.

"I don't go by looks, Disbrow," Mac said with a flinty edge to his voice.

"Oh, right, you still expect your 'God' to rescue you, don't you?"

"You would do well to turn to Him too. You aren't faring too well by your own devices."

Disbrow mumbled to himself as he drew two skeletons in the dirt floor with his finger. When a guard walked by a few seconds later, Mac stood. "How long will we be held in here?"

"This may be your last stop." The scruffy-looking fellow grinned at Mac, displaying no more than four teeth. "I've heard rumors."

"What rumors?"

"Ask the other cellmates," he said with a sneer.

Mac gripped the bars. "What other cellmates?"

"The ones all over the floor!" The guard laughed. Mac stumbled backward at the man's noxious breath and then watched him walk away.

Mac's heart sank. Perhaps this *was* the end of the road, how his life was supposed to end. *Where are the king and his soldiers? Surely the king knows our plight by now?* He shuddered down to his bones as he asked himself the next question: *Where is God?*

The whole ordeal had tested Mac's faith several times, but for the first time since he arrived, his faith hung by a silken thread so tenuous the weight of a spider could break it. He grasped the bars of the jail cell and closed his eyes, feeling his legs grow as weak as water.

Then his heart stirred. Joshua 1:5 surfaced in his mind: "No one will be able to stand up against you all the days of your life. As I was with Moses, so I will be with you; I will never leave you nor forsake you." A surge of energy ran through Mac, and the vigor returned to his legs. He drew himself up, opening his eyes.

"Thank you, Father," Mac whispered. "I won't doubt You again."

"What's that, mate?" Disbrow stretched his legs and folded his arms. "I didn't hear ya."

"Take heart, Disbrow! You will witness the power and faithfulness of my God!"

The hint of a smile appeared on Disbrow's face.

# Chapter Fourteen

**B**y noon, Sean and Andy had covered more than half the distance to Alexander's lair. The sight of the tall mountain growing closer fueled their desire to cover as much ground as possible before sunset. Although steel gray clouds rolled across the sky, intermittent beams of sunlight broke through and warmed their faces.

While traveling through a patch of forest, they paused by a river bank to refill their flasks and let Saber and Paladin drink. As Sean crouched beside the frigid water, Andy screamed. Sean looked up to see him stumble back from a fallen tree stretched out across half the river. Then Andy tripped over his own foot and fell.

"What is it?" Sean stood and walked toward Andy.

As he neared the tree, a flash of white caught his eye—a body tangled in the branches. Ribbons of bloated white flesh and blue veins had been torn away, exposing threads of muscle and glistening organs. Brown hair still clung to the scalp, but Sean could not see its face. Then the reek of decaying flesh hit him, and his stomach spasmed. He stumbled away and vomited onto the bank until nothing more came out. Then he sat down hard and shook.

After a few minutes, Andy's thin voice reached Sean. "What happened to him?"

Sean noticed deep gouges in the tree trunk and remembered Nafaar's silver talons. Andy turned to look at him. Not wanting to scare the boy, Sean took a few deep breaths. "I think he drowned. Maybe some animals … got to him after he froze to death in the water."

His stomach rolled again, but Sean put his head between his knees and rocked back and forth for a few moments. Saber brushed against him with a low purr, but Andy's soft sobs prompted the dragon to tend to his smaller companion. After a while, Sean's throat no longer burned, and his stomach's soreness faded. Still shaking, he looked up at Paladin, keeping his eyes away from the body. Then he stood.

"Let's get out of here, Andy."

Without a word, the boys left the river behind and returned to the forest. A few hours later, they happened upon a small stone house with a thatched roof. A thin column of smoke rose from the chimney, and shadows shifted behind one of the windows. Toward the rear corner of the homestead stood an old barn.

Tethering Paladin and Saber to a tree near a small pond, the boys approached the house.

"Hello?" Sean called. "Is anyone in?"

No one responded. Andy strode up to the heavy wooden door and knocked. Still no response. After a moment, he pounded on the door.

"Don't, Andy!" Sean grabbed his arm. "We're looking to make friends, not enemies."

But the door flew open, and a tall man with a thick shock of gray hair charged out. He wielded a crossbow with a long, sharp arrow pointed at them.

"Whoa, whoa!" Sean said. He jumped back, pulling Andy with him. "Easy with that! We come in peace, sir!" They held up their hands.

The man jabbed the arrow in Sean's direction. "Then knock in a peaceable manner!"

"Please forgive us; we mean no harm." Sean lowered his hands. "We exhausted our food supply and hoped to buy some food from you."

"First thing's first. Lay your sword and crossbow on that bench." The man pointed his arrow to the left. "I'll not have strangers in my home with weapons."

Sean and Andy followed his orders and then returned to his doorstep. The man lowered his crossbow. "Who are you, from whence do you come, and what is your destination?"

"My name is Sean Delbridge. I'm from Maryport. This is Andy Brandt, and he's from—" Turning to Andy, Sean asked, "Where are you from? You never told me."

Resting his free hand on his hip, the man raised an eyebrow. "Don't quite have your stories lined up yet, eh boys?"

"I'm originally from York, sir." Andy said.

"We are on a journey to find Alexander," Sean said. "I'm sure you know of him, since you live so close to him."

"If you speak of Alexander the dragon, we have not seen evidence that he still lives. We have seen dragons above the hills, but none as large as Alexander."

Paladin whinnied, and the man looked toward the pond. Saber perched on a tree branch, his tether wound around the trunk as he gripped the bark with his talons. The man's eyes widened as he stared at Saber, then he raised his crossbow.

"No!" Andy stepped in front of him. "Please, sir, that's my Saber. He's harmless!"

"What is a dragon doing on my property?" The man lowered his weapon again.

"He's very docile, sir." Sean said. "He is Andy's companion and transportation."

The man's demeanor softened, and a warm smile appeared. "All right, boys. My name is Henry Gregg. I'm sorry about my rough edges, but these are dangerous times, and one cannot take unnecessary risks." He turned toward the door. "Come enjoy a meal Mrs. Gregg and my daughter are preparing as we speak." With his hand on the doorknob, he looked back over his shoulder and added with a smile, "At no charge to you."

Sean stepped through the door and was welcomed by an aroma that reminded him of his mother's cooking. His mouth watered as the scents of herbs, spices, and tea filled the air. Mrs. Gregg, petite with brown hair, stood over a wood-burning stove as she added a portion of meat to the frying pan. Then she turned and nodded with a smile.

"Good day, Mrs. Gregg. My name is Sean Delbridge, and this is Andy Brandt."

Andy, already into his second bow, smiled at Mrs. Gregg. "Thank you so much for having us, ma'am. You have a very nice home."

"You are welcome, and thank you," she replied.

A fireplace crackled nearby, and a young lady prepared beans and potatoes at the table. She looked up with deep brown eyes.

"I'm Victoria." She smiled.

Sean stared. She blushed and looked back down at the food, her raven hair spilling over her shoulders. Andy kicked Sean's ankle, and Sean straightened up, his face burning.

"It is a plea … pleasure to make your acquaintance."

Andy rolled his eyes while Mr. and Mrs. Gregg grinned at each other. Mr. Gregg pulled two more chairs to the table. "All right, boys. Have a seat. Sean, while we're waiting, why don't you tell us why you want to find Alexander."

Despite the stove and fireplace, a shiver ran down Sean's arms. He explained his situation as Mrs. Gregg and Victoria finished preparing the meal. Mr. Gregg folded his arms and rested his elbows against the table.

"We've heard reports of what's been happening around the country, and Lady Silver's reputation is known in even our remote hamlet." He unfolded his arms as the ladies placed bowls and plates of food on the table. "We have taken precautionary measures ourselves by keeping our livestock in the barn and only venturing outside when necessary. I can only guess what other evil Silver plans. You may notice it is a bit chilly in our home." He motioned towards the hearth. "We only build small fires to avoid drawing attention to our home with heavy chimney smoke."

Sean nodded, although the smell of the hot potatoes and meat drew his eyes away.

Victoria poured tea into his cup, avoiding his gaze. "I am sorry about your father, Sean."

Sean, tongue-tied and blushing, lowered his gaze and barely managed a thank you.

Mrs. Gregg sat. "Shall we pray over our meal?"

"We thank You for the meal we are about to receive, Lord," Mr. Gregg prayed. "We also pray You guide and protect these young men. In our Savior's name we pray. Amen."

Andy was filling his plate before the "amen" left Mr. Gregg's lips.

"Thank you, Mr. Gregg," Sean said, glaring at Andy while the latter sank his teeth into a helping of lamb, chewed, swallowed, and then shoveled a forkful of vegetables into his mouth. After swallowing, he smiled at Mrs. Gregg.

"Delicious meal. We may just have to stop by on our way back!"

Sean stared at Andy, but all three Greggs laughed.

"Yes, the food is delicious," Sean said. "But I'm afraid we won't be coming back this way anytime soon. If I can't find Alexander or get him to help us, I will find my father myself."

Mr. and Mrs. Gregg looked at each other, and Victoria frowned. Andy, on the other hand swallowed a few gulps of water and then brought a second helping of lamb onto his plate.

Mr. Gregg placed his fork beside his plate. "Is that wise, son? I'm sure the king can deal with this crisis."

Sean slid his plate forward, resting his elbows on the table. "I hope you're right, sir, but I can't just do nothing. If Alexander can't help, I'm sure the king will need all the help he can get."

They ate in silence for a few minutes. After the Greggs cleared their plates, Sean scooted his chair back. "Can we help you clean the dishes, Mrs. Gregg?"

"No, no. We know you have a mountain to conquer, so we don't want to hold you back. But thank you for offering."

"I hope we don't appear rude, but we do have to push off."

Andy remained in his seat, eating his second piece of cherry pie.

Victoria's eyes sparkled as she watched him enjoy the dessert. "Andy, would you like a third piece of my pie?" She pressed a finger to her lips to suppress her laughter. "I baked two."

Sean folded his arms and shook his head.

Andy looked up. "No thanks," he said through a mouthful of pie. "But hopefully, we'll be back for more soon."

"I would like—*we* would like that very much," Victoria said, smiling at Sean.

Mrs. Gregg grabbed a cloth and spread it out on the table. "Boys, take what's left of this meat and pie with you." She placed the food in the center of the cloth and wrapped it. "It's not much, but it should get you through to tomorrow morning."

Mr. Gregg stood beside his wife and smiled at the boys. "Would you gentlemen like a few old sweaters of mine to take with you, just in case? You don't look too warmly dressed for the chilly weather coming your way."

Sean held up his hand. "Oh, we couldn't—"

"I would feel better if you did, and they are old garments I don't wear anymore."

Sean nodded. "That is very kind of you. I hope we can repay you someday."

Mrs. Gregg handed the bundle of food to Sean. "Come back and visit us safe and sound. That will be payment enough."

Mr. Gregg returned with the sweaters. "May the Lord be with you boys. If you run into any trouble, you are always welcome here."

"We appreciate that," Sean said.

Andy set his fork down. "Thank you," he said, admiring his new sweater.

Rubbing their swollen stomachs, Sean and Andy walked outside and took their weapons from the bench outside. After only a few steps, Sean turned to Victoria, who stood with her parents at the door.

"I hope to try some of your cherry pie again one of these days, Victoria."

Victoria smiled and nodded.

As Sean and Andy approached Paladin and Saber, Sean whispered, "What did you think of Victoria?"

"Very pretty. The food was delicious. Do you think we can come back for more?"

Sean shook his head.

"What's the matter with you?" Andy asked.

"You ate so much of their food I'm surprised you could make it through the door!"

"Well, at least I kept my eyes on my food. Why didn't you just propose to her in the middle of our meal?"

Sean looked at Paladin and grinned. "She is beautiful, isn't she?" He gathered Paladin's reins. "Papa once told me a person's eyes are a portal into the soul, and she had the most heavenly eyes."

Andy rolled his eyes as he untethered Saber. The dragon shook his head, then sat back and scratched his neck with his hind foot like a dog.

"I know what you're going to talk about all day," Andy said.

Sean mounted Paladin and then pulled Andy up with him. "Let's go find Alexander."

# Chapter Fifteen

**M**ac hadn't realized how accustomed he had grown to the discordant sounds of the colliery—the shouting guards, the clanging pickaxes—until it all ceased. Mac and Disbrow looked at each other from across the jail cell. Pulling himself up from the floor, Mac walked to the bars and, looking left and right, motioned to Disbrow to remain still. He closed his eyes and listened. After a few moments, distant shouts of "back to work!" reached Mac's ears, and the sounds resumed.

As Mac turned back to his corner, Disbrow pointed. "Look, mate! Someone's coming!"

A single oil lamp hung on the wall across from their cell, casting a faint light that sent long shadows across the chiseled stone walls. Since morning, a number of guards had passed them, including one who delivered cold soup and a bucket of foul-smelling drinking water. Their sneers and taunts evoked no response from Mac and Disbrow, but the guards still kept their arms and hands beyond Disbrow's reach.

But the guards who now approached wore clean armor and came equipped with swords, not whips. Fear rose in Mac's belly, and he stepped back. She was a tall woman with silvery-white hair that fell below her shoulders, and she towered over the six armed guards who accompanied her. She reached up and tapped her claw-like nails on the only piece of jewelry she wore: a necklace strung with silver-plated talons.

"Good afternoon, gentlemen. I am Lady Silver." She fixed her black eyes on Mac, and a smirk lifted her high cheek bones. "It is particularly satisfying to meet you, Mr. Delbridge. My, my. You have certainly made your presence known during your little stay. Is there anything I can get for you? A cup of tea, perhaps?"

"There is nothing I want from you." Mac took a deep breath, willing his speeding heart to slow, and prayed for the courage to stand his ground.

Lady Silver clucked her tongue. "Now, now. The last thing I want is for there to be hard feelings between us, Mr. Delbridge."

Behind Lady Silver, a tall, slender man emerged. Shadows flickered across his lined, weathered face. Then, sweeping his silver ponytail over one shoulder, he stood with his legs apart and folded his arms.

"You are in no position to dismiss Lady Silver's generosity," he said.

Lady Silver glanced at the man, and then looked back at Mac. "Malek is right, Mr. Delbridge. You should consider your situation more thoughtfully."

Mac glared at Lady Silver's henchman, and then turned back to the woman who smirked at him. "Your rule is coming to a close, Silver—"

"That's 'Lady Silver' to you!" She narrowed her eyes. "And that is high talk for someone who will soon make an appearance on Nafaar's dinner platter!"

Mac refused to let fear overpower him this time. "You can place me on any platter you so desire, lady!"

"Don't you dare talk to me like—"

"I'm not finished!" Mac roared. The guards stepped forward, weapons ready. "Even if you succeed in eliminating me, God's judgment over you will prevail! And make no mistake. Other men in this mine will make their voices heard!"

Mac folded his arms and glared at Lady Silver. Behind him came a scraping sound, then Disbrow appeared beside him. He crossed his arms as well. Lady Silver stared back, her cheeks flushed, but her eyes remained hard and cold.

"Mr. Delbridge, even your God cannot prevent what I have in store for you and your fat friend."

She turned and strode away. Malek and the guards followed, and Mac wondered how much time he had left on this earth.

\* \* \* \*

By the time Sean and Andy approached the stream near the base of Alexander's mountain, only a sliver of the sun remained above the horizon. Sean knew better than to try to negotiate the mountain in the dark. He sighed.

"The light is almost gone, Andy. We'll have to make camp here and then start again at the break of dawn." He scanned the mountainside. "It will take at least two hours to get to the top, and I don't want to introduce myself to the largest dragon in England when it's pitch black!"

Saber chirped. When Andy looked at him, the dragon bounced like an excited dog, pumping his half-spread wings. Then the powerful sound of beating wings swept overhead, and the boys looked up to see the tail of a large dragon disappear into the shadows at the top of the mountain. Sean stared after it for a moment, then turned and hurried toward the trees by the stream. Andy followed with Saber in tow.

"Do you think it's Alexander?" Andy whispered.

"I don't know."

As the sun set, it gave the stream an orange tint before darkness turned the forest gray. A cold breeze blew through the trees, and thick clouds allowed only a pale light from the crescent moon.

Listening for any other dragons, Sean had second thoughts about dragging Andy into this adventure. After all, Andy was still closer to boyhood than manhood.

"Andy, it may not be a good idea to continue with me," he said.

95

"What do you mean?"

"Maybe you should go back to the Greggs' and stay there until this is over. I don't want to see you get hurt."

"Look, Sean, I owe you my life, but my vow to help you is no longer just an obligation. I'm having a good time, and I'm not going anywhere except up this mountain with you."

Sean smiled. "You are pretty stubborn, aren't you?"

Andy chuckled. "You have no idea."

"Well then, I think the coast is clear, but stay hidden." Sean stepped out from under the tree. "Let's take off the saddles, eat some of Mrs. Gregg's lamb and cherry pie, and then go to sleep. I have a feeling we've got an interesting day ahead of us."

Andy nodded. "Sounds good to me."

While Paladin grazed, Sean and Andy ate their fill of the lamb and cherry pie, then fed the rest to Saber. Sean's full stomach sent waves of blissful weariness over him, and he smiled through half-lidded eyes. He and Andy wrapped themselves in their blankets, and Andy tucked himself up against Saber where the dragon lay beneath a tree.

"You can sleep here too, Sean. Saber won't mind."

As Sean crawled over, Saber glanced at him. In the darkness, the dragon's eyes glowed as though phosphorescent. Ignoring the animal's cat-like eyeshine, Sean propped himself against Saber's side, which radiated a surprising amount of heat for a scaly animal like a dragon. Saber curled around the pair and draped one enormous wing over them, blocking the cold breeze.

Through a gap above him, Sean watched the clouds thin and shift north. A black sky with its bright stars opened up before their eyes.

"Isn't it beautiful?" Andy asked with a yawn.

"Yes, it is." Sean yawned too. "My father and I used to sit at the barn's loft window on nights like this. We'd lean back and watch for shooting stars, seeing who could count the most."

"I wonder if my parents are up there."

"Of course they are. You'll see them again in Heaven."

"I don't know about that. I suspect God's had it with waiting for me to come back."

"I don't believe that, Andy. You have a good heart. You've just stepped back for awhile because of the pain you've suffered. But the Lord has never left you." Sean looked at Andy. "He loves you more than you can understand. He's waiting for you to return to Him. He is only a prayer away."

Andy sniffled.

"Do you mind if I pray, Andy?"

"No, I guess not."

Sean looked back up at the stars. "Lord, the book of Psalms says You are not only near the brokenhearted, but that You also heal them. I pray You continue to show Andy how much You love him. Help him, Father. I don't know what tomorrow will bring, but help and protect us—and please watch over my parents. In Jesus' name we pray, amen."

Out of the corner of his eye, Sean saw Andy's lips move. With a smile, Sean wrapped his blanket more snugly around himself and closed his eyes.

# Chapter Sixteen

Without any ability to track the time, Mac wondered if twelve hours had passed or twelve minutes. Night was upon them, he presumed, because the sounds in the mine had ceased. After the scripture had filled Mac's heart earlier, he had been biding his time with the quiet confidence that God was with him. Disbrow, however, slumped in a corner with his back against the bars.

"Are you ready, Disbrow?"

Disbrow raised his heavy eyes to Mac. "Ready to die? No, are you?"

"I don't mean that. Are you ready to give your heart to the Lord?"

Disbrow hesitated. "I go to church every once in awhile—when I'm not here on holiday."

Mac smiled at Disbrow's curmudgeonly façade and lifted himself up off the floor, moving to sit closer to the brooding giant. "That doesn't get you to Heaven, Disbrow."

"People with my background don't go to heaven."

"What do you mean?"

Disbrow stared at the oil lamp on the wall. "Most of the men in my family were miners; my father, grandfather … it's been miserable. My father told me I wasn't good enough—" He swallowed several times. "He told me I wasn't good enough to do anything else."

Mac stayed silent as Disbrow wiped his eyes. After a few seconds, the larger man took a deep breath and sighed. "I have an older brother, David, who escaped the mines. He moved to London to go to school and lived with my aunt and uncle. My father sent him what little money he had to finish his education." Disbrow looked down at his feet. "David is a doctor now. I haven't seen him since he left. And I never married; most women are afraid of me. I had no place else to go except the colliery."

"What about your mother?" Mac asked.

Beyond the cell, a large, gray rat emerged from a small opening at the base of the stone wall. It scurried into their cell, pausing to sniff. Mac studied the rat, and Disbrow shifted his weight, prompting the rodent to dash back into the darkness. He chuckled, shaking his head.

"If you ever tasted my father's cooking, Delbridge, that little fellow might not look so bad as this evening's supper."

Mac grinned as Disbrow leaned down with a grunt, resting his elbow on the hard floor. "You asked about my mother. She left my father when I was seventeen. She wanted to stay long enough to raise me, and then she just couldn't take it anymore. My father is a brutal man. I learned later that she went to live with an aunt on the coast near Newcastle."

Mac rose from his seat and knelt beside Disbrow, placing his hand on his cellmate's shoulder. "Disbrow, your earthly father may have failed you, but I want you to know you have a heavenly father who loves you unconditionally. He wants to help you."

Disbrow wiped beads of sweat from his forehead with his sleeve. "God knows I need the help. What can I do?"

"The Bible says in the book of John, chapter three, verse sixteen, 'For God so loved the world that He gave His one and only Son, that whoever believes in Him shall not perish but have eternal life.' The first step in coming to God is to admit you are a sinner; we all are. But when we ask God to forgive us, and when we accept His son Jesus Christ as our savior, He will forgive us and He promises to give us eternal life in Heaven. It's really that simple. And one more thing, which may be the hardest ... you must forgive everyone who hurt you—including your father."

Disbrow shook his head. "I don't know if I can do that."

"I know. But God says He cannot forgive us if we cannot forgive others. Because of His love for you, Christ cancelled the debt of your sin by dying on a cross for you, and now He commands us to forgive the sins committed against us. If you decide to forgive your father, God will help you forgive him. The Bible also says that when we invite Jesus into our lives, His presence in our hearts makes it possible for us to offer unconditional love and forgiveness to others, even those who hurt us."

Disbrow looked into Mac's eyes. "It sounds almost too good to be true. So let me get this straight: I just ask God to forgive me for my sins, and I accept Christ as my savior? And then I will go to Heaven if things don't go so well here?"

"If you are sincere, yes. You will be forgiven and receive eternal life."

"I guess I have some praying to do then."

Mac patted Disbrow on his massive shoulder and then returned to his corner.

"Oh, just one more thing, Delbridge … thanks for this morning."

"You're welcome, and call me Mac."

"All right, Mac. You can call me by my nickname."

"What's that?"

"Tiny."

Mac chuckled as he lay down on the floor. After standing and swinging his pickax for days, he took advantage of this opportunity to relax. "I should have guessed. After you pray, get some sleep. We may need our strength soon."

# Chapter Seventeen

T ucked against Saber's warm torso, Sean did not wake until morning. When he did, a clear blue sky stretched above him beyond the translucent gray membranes of Saber's wing. Vigorous splashing made him glance down the stream—where a dozen or so large gray dragons bathed. Andy crouched against Saber's side and watched the serpents, while Paladin grazed in the shadows. Saber stared at the dragons.

A few serpents thrust their long snouts into the water, emerged with large fish, and then tossed them into the air and caught them in their gullet. Soon, every dragon followed suit, moving up and down that area of the creek and catching their fill. After a few minutes, the dragons flung additional fish onto the creek bank, and after they had thrown a hundred or so fish onto the grass, the dragons flapped their wings and rose above the creek, spraying water everywhere. The dragons then snatched up as many fish as their mouths and talons could fit and pumped their wings until they disappeared over the top of the mountain.

"That was incredible!" Sean said. "I've never seen anything like it."

103

"Oh, that was nothing." Andy sniffed. "You should see Saber fish."

"I wonder if they're Alexander's companions. What were they doing with the extra fish?"

"Maybe they have babies to feed."

"Yeah, probably. That reminds me, Andy. Micah told me to take a gift of food to offer Alexander. Do you think Saber could help us catch a string of fish?"

"No problem. Between Saber and my crossbow, we'll deliver as many as you need."

Sean arched an eyebrow. "You fish with a crossbow?"

Andy smiled and stood. "Observe."

As Sean crouched and watched, Andy strutted like a barnyard rooster to collect his crossbow from under the tree. After placing an arrow across its frame, he stepped to the edge of the creek, scanning it for a target. Suddenly the arrow shot forward.

"Darn it!" Andy kicked the ground. "I must be off my game. I hit his tail."

Sean threw his head back and laughed. "I can't believe it, Andy! I would have been lucky to hit the water!"

Saber rolled to his stomach and tucked his wings, then sat back on his haunches and watched. Andy put down his crossbow, pulled off his boots and socks, hiked his trouser legs, and stepped into the creek. "Whoa, that's cold!" He crossed his arms and shivered, then reached down and turned to Sean with his arrow in one hand and the fish in his other.

"How did you learn to shoot like that?"

Andy stepped out of the creek. "It's called mastering the art of survival. I didn't have a choice if I was going to eat! Saber makes it easier for me, though. He's a natural-born catcher of fish and small game."

As Andy walked back onto the bank, Saber bounded past him and leaped into the water, sending a sheet of water splashing down on Andy. He flinched and turned.

"Hey!"

Saber paddled around in the creek, dipping his head beneath the current. Within seconds, he tossed his head up with a silver fish thrashing in his jaws. The dragon gave it a few hard chomps, then tossed it back down his throat and gulped. After about twenty minutes, Saber had supplied enough fish to fill the stringer.

Sean eyed the fish. "I wish we could cook some for ourselves, but a fire might draw attention. Let's see what's left in our satchels and then start moving before these fish spoil."

\* \* \* \*

Disbrow slept well, but Mac did not; between the chill and thoughts about his wife and son's well-being, he only slept an hour or so.

105

"Good morning, mate!" Disbrow declared. "Did you get any sleep?"

"Not much," Mac grumbled.

"I'm hungry."

"Something tells me the ham and eggs won't arrive anytime soon."

At that moment, a guard walked by and caught the last of their conversation. "A glorious morning to you blokes!" The four-toothed guard smiled. "I'm afraid your personal chef hasn't prepared anything for you this morning, but I understand a last meal will be delivered later on." He rubbed his hands together. "Now, we don't want you two to despair; your troubles will soon be over." His laughter trailed off as he walked past their cell.

Disbrow shook his head. "Things look a bit sour, eh? Hey, what's with the long face? You told me God's in control, didn't you? Has anything changed since last night?"

Mac sat up and shook his head. "You're right, Tiny. I'm sorry. I didn't get much sleep."

"That's all right, Mac. Look, worst case is we'll go to Heaven today, right?" Disbrow beamed. His child-like faith lifted Mac's spirits, and he smiled back.

"I couldn't have picked a better cellmate, Tiny."

Disbrow tipped his imaginary hat towards Mac. "My pleasure. Now, I know you're the teacher and I'm the student, but shouldn't we pray?"

Mac stared at Disbrow. "Perhaps you should take over as teacher. You are right again!"

Grasping Disbrow's hand and bowing in the darkness, Mac led the prayer. They asked for peace, grace, and strength to face the day.

# Chapter Eighteen

After eating the last two blueberry muffins, Sean and Andy followed the stream until they found a shallow area to cross. With the sun at their backs and Saber and Paladin by their side, the boys ascended the mountain. They struggled to thread a consistent pathway up the rough terrain. The autumn wind had stripped the few trees free of leaves, leaving Sean and Andy exposed to the sunlight that still burned despite the chilly air.

Pausing to catch his breath, Sean sat on a boulder. "We're open game to any dragons."

"I was thinking the same thing. We better hope we aren't near any baby dragons. No creature is as ferocious as a mother dragon protecting her young."

Sean took a deep breath and sighed. "We have no choice."

The boys drank from their flasks and then offered Paladin and Saber cupped handfuls.

"Well, let's go." Sean slapped his knee and stood. "Another hour should get us to the top."

The sun climbed during the final leg of their trek, and Sean no longer shivered. "Almost there," he said, nearly out of breath. "There's the crest."

After a few minutes, the terrain leveled off, and Sean and Andy reached the top. Andy gasped. "Look, Sean! I've never seen anything like it in all my life!"

Sean stared with his mouth agape. Before them rose mountain peaks of varying heights forming a huge ring, with more than fifty dragon lairs carved out of their sides. The sight that stole their breath, however, was the great gathering of dragons. Some lounged in the sun at the mouth of their lairs while others bathed in a lagoon at the base of the mountains. At the water's edge lay the partially submerged skeleton of a dragon.

"That must be Evangeline, Alexander's mate," Sean whispered.

Andy nodded and then looked around. "That's strange. Most of them appear to be adult bulls; very few females or juveniles."

"They must be Alexander's army, still loyal," Sean said. "I'll wager this means he is still alive!"

To their left near the top of the tallest mountain, two dragons perched above the entranceway to a huge cavern near a waterfall.

Sean pointed. "Look! That must be Alexander's lair!"

Andy nodded. "I think you're right. It's three times bigger than the others. But how will we ever get to Alexander?"

"God's grace," Sean said with a nervous smile. "Now let's tether Paladin and Saber behind these trees and see what kind of reception we get."

Andy looked at Saber, then back to Sean. "What if they find Saber? Do you think they'll attack him, since he's not one of them? And what if they find Paladin?"

"I'm sure Paladin will be fine here. I don't know about Saber, though."

"Saber probably will not like me leaving him here. He will want to protect me, especially with all these other dragons around."

Glancing out at the swooping dragons, Sean looked back at the much smaller Saber. "He's young, so he's not a big threat. Maybe they will leave him alone."

"I think so. And if they see us with him, maybe they won't consider us a threat either."

Sean secured Paladin to a rocky outcropping, where the horse rested in the ledge's shade.

"Let's take our flasks," Andy said. "Hopefully, we can refill them at that waterfall down there."

"Good idea. And one more thing," Sean said. "We need to leave our weapons here."

Andy stared at Sean. "Are you daft?"

"We cannot pose any threat. I'm only taking the fish and Micah's shofar." Sean studied his friend. "I wouldn't blame you if you stayed here."

"You still don't know me very well. Let's go."

Only moments later as they made their way towards Alexander's lair, Andy slipped on loose gravel and fell. The loud scraping sound and Andy's yelp echoed throughout the canyon below. Within seconds, the thunderous sound of beating wings filled the air as a host of dragons rushed toward them. Andy shot up off the ground, and both he and Sean froze. Saber pressed himself against the ground and flattened his ears, staring around him. The massive dragons blocked out the sunlight as they surrounded Sean and Andy, perching in trees or atop large boulders. Their deep growls hummed in the air, and Saber returned the growls with his own.

After a few moments of fervent prayer, waves of peace swept over Sean. His pounding heart slowed, and he took a deep breath. Andy closed his eyes and moved his lips.

"It will be all right," Sean whispered.

The boys stood staring at the ground for several minutes. Then one dragon's shadow rose as it flew away, and more shadows disappeared. Sean looked up into the sun, then over at Andy.

"Are you all right?"

Andy looked at Sean. "It's a miracle! What happened?"

"I guess they don't consider us a threat. Or maybe they don't like the taste of humans. Did you hurt yourself?"

"No, and sorry I announced our arrival like that."

"Did I see you praying?"

"Yes," Andy answered, with the expression of one who just got caught stealing a pie out of the baker's window. "It seemed like the thing to do."

"I'm glad you did. We were in a bit of a tight spot there."

"Let's carry on, shall we?"

# Chapter Nineteen

Sean smiled and walked ahead of Andy, following the trail that wound down and then up, left and right. They stayed out in the open so they would not surprise the sentries. Sean wondered how they would reach the other side of the waterfall that cascaded down the hill between them and their destination.

Andy stopped and looked across the waterfall. Then he turned and tightened the straps on Saber's saddle.

"Oh no," Sean stepped back. "No, no. We aren't using Saber to get across."

Andy shrugged. "We have no other choice, do we? You need Alexander's help to find your father, right? Well, if you want to reach him, your only way over there is on Saber's back."

As Andy pulled himself up into the saddle, Sean looked back at the waterfall that crashed down into the rocky basin below. With tons of water power behind it, the cascade could knock even Saber down into the rocks if he veered too close.

*No other way across ...*

"Just watch what I do," Andy said. He fastened the straps around his waist and legs, placed his feet in the stirrups, and bent down. "Let's go, Saber!"

The dragon spread his expansive wings and pumped them. The gusts ruffled Sean's brown hair as Saber rose a few meters off the ground, then dropped over the ledge and navigated around the waterfall. Its mist drenched Andy, but he clung to Saber's shoulders. They reached the other side and touched down.

Andy turned to Sean and moved his mouth, but the waterfall's roar drowned his words. As he unfastened the straps and climbed off Saber, Sean's stomach churned. He didn't risk peeking out over the ledge for fear of losing his balance and falling off. Instead, he pressed himself back against the hill.

The flapping of leathery wings made Sean look up. Saber landed before him and met his gaze, but Sean's arms felt encased in lead and his legs rooted to the ground.

*Move.*

Sean forced one leg forward, then the other, until he reached Saber. But he could not bring himself to climb onto the dragon, even though Saber now crouched to give Sean easy access to the saddle. Closing his eyes, Sean prayed for the strength to get it over with.

Seconds passed. Saber peered back at Sean, who stood with his head tilted down. The crashing waterfall faded into a dull roar. Then Sean looked up. His heart slowed, and he took deep, measured breaths as he reached out and touched the misty saddle. With trembling

114

hands, he pulled himself up into the saddle and focused on every detail of the task at hand. He fastened the straps so tightly his legs throbbed, and then he slid his feet into the stirrups.

*No turning back now.*

Leaning down and gripping Saber's slick shoulder blades as best he could, Sean clung to the dragon and waited. Saber glanced back at him again, then crouched lower and pumped his wings. Each beat blew Sean's hair upward, and the ground dropped away—as did Sean's stomach. The pair rose and fell with the rhythmic wing beats like a ship riding over ocean waves. Then, Saber tilted his body and thrust himself off the ledge.

The waterfall opened up below Sean, plunging for what looked like miles. Sean flattened himself against Saber and dug every inch of his fingers into the dragon's pebbled skin. They rose toward Andy on the other side, and before Sean could look down again, Saber sailed up onto the hill and landed with a soft thump beside Andy.

"How did you like it?" He grinned as he unfastened Sean's straps. Sean slumped against the dragon, his arms hanging limp while he tried to catch his breath. Finally, he pulled his feet out of the stirrups and slid off Saber. His knees buckled when he landed, and he stumbled backward to sit down on a patch of damp grass, his shirt and hair dripping.

Andy laughed. "You don't look too good. Here, let me fill your flask. You sit there." He filled their flasks with the cold, crystalline water, then handed Sean his refilled flask. Sean looked at Andy's muddy clothing, then glanced down to see grime smeared down his chest and legs from where he had clung to Saber.

"I'm sure Alexander will be impressed," he grumbled, wiping the muck.

Andy slapped Sean's shoulder. "Let's go. We're almost there."

Sean stood, and they both climbed toward Alexander's lair. The two dragon sentries came into full view, sitting erect and watching the two boys with a low hiss. As Saber followed low to the ground like a cautious cat, he gave a quiet growl.

Within moments, they stood before the entrance below the two sentries. Beyond the mouth of the huge lair, shadows gave way into an abyss of darkness. Fresh fish littered the entrance, and Sean wrinkled his nose at their strong smell.

The hissing subsided as the dragon sentries stepped off their perches and descended to opposite ends of the lair's terrace.

"No sudden moves," Sean whispered.

"Thanks for the advice," Andy replied. "I was just about to start dancing."

As Sean stepped forward, the air behind them filled with thrumming dragon wings. He glanced back to see every dragon within sight flying to them, their huge bodies casting shadows across the boys. A light silver one landed within reach of Sean, and a cream-colored one no larger than Saber lingered near Andy. The dragons assembled in a half circle behind the boys.

Trying to speak without moving his lips, Andy whispered, "Sean, if we get out of this alive, can we call it even between us?"

"Things were never uneven."

"What do we do now?"

Sean slipped the leather strap of Micah's shofar from around his left shoulder and raised it to his parched lips. No sound came forth. Shifting to his water flask, Sean took a long sip. Then, he raised the horn to his mouth again and blew, this time releasing a clear, strong bugle-like call.

A blast of fire exploded from inside the lair. It reached within a meter from where Sean and Andy stood, and the heat reddened their faces. Sean fell back onto his rear, and Andy fainted, crumpling to the ground. For a moment, Sean thought he had angered Alexander, and he froze amidst the dragons. Chills ran up his wet arms, but he climbed back to his feet and balled his hands into fists, feeling their rush of adrenaline. He peered into the cave.

Two great luminous eyes the size of cannonballs turned to look at him. The ground shook as the majestic dragon drew nearer.

Sean's heartbeat quickened. "Please, Alexander, we mean no harm."

Footsteps crunched on the rocky floor, and a massive clawed foot landed in the sunlight. Sean lifted his gaze, keeping his head bowed. The huge chest of the dragon, as wide and tall as the bow of a ship and covered with gleaming scales of gold almost blinded him. Hot jets of air grazed the back of Sean's neck, tinged with the smell of smoke. A throaty growl broke the silence.

He stood in Alexander's own lair, his mouth wide open. No fairytale or dragon legend had prepared him for the massive size of this beast.

While absorbing the shock of the experience, the weight of Sean's mission bore down on him. He had traveled so far on foot, on horseback, even on another dragon's back, just to reach this lair. And now he had not only found Alexander alive, but he stood at the dragon's feet. He had the dragon's attention. And the life of his father, his mother, and thousands of citizens of England depended upon what Sean would do next.

The pressure swelled in Sean until tears stung his eyes and his nose burned. Then sobs hit him, and he collapsed to his knees before Alexander, hot tears streaming down his chilled cheeks. He no longer felt any fear, but he also no longer felt courage. He'd finally surrendered the last scintilla of stubborn will to God.

Alexander's growling softened. Sean leaned back and stared out at the dragon's blurred chest. The massive head and gleaming eyes hung above, also a blur.

Through his tears, Sean said in a tense voice, "Micah sent me."

Alexander cocked his head and stared down at Sean.

"I come for your help. My father has been kidnapped … by Nafaar."

A deep, rumbling growl filled the air, and Alexander's chest swelled. Lest the dragon storm away, Sean spoke quickly.

"Nafaar is not dead, Alexander. He continues in his service to Lady Silver."

Alexander's growl deepened until it ricocheted off the cavern walls.

"Micah said you might be able to help me." Taking a deep breath, Sean wiped his face, smearing a bit of mud across it as he did so. Andy groaned next to him and rolled his head, still unconscious. Glancing down at his friend and then back to Alexander's shadow, Sean pulled the fish off the stringer and tossed them into the scattered pile before Alexander.

"Please accept these as a gift from Micah and me. I hope they are still fresh enough."

The growling ceased, and Alexander lowered his massive head. His breath scattered bits of rock and dust at his feet as he ate the fish. When the muffled crunching of tiny bones faded, the great dragon nodded toward him. And then, Alexander turned and disappeared into his lair.

Sean watched him leave, then sighed and sat down. *I did it. I found Alexander. Now what?*

The sounds of shuffling behind him made Sean glance back. A blue dragon, the smallest of them all, approached Andy and Saber. A black stripe ran from the bridge of its snout and across its cheek down the length of its body. Saber stared at the dragon, then crouched over

119

Andy and lowered his head. A deep hiss erupted from Saber's throat at the larger dragon, making it pause. Then it swept its black eyes to Sean and, after a few seconds, turned and climbed up onto a boulder.

Andy, still lying where he had fainted, moved his arm, scraping the rocky ground. Then he groaned, rolled his head, and opened his eyes. As Sean helped him to his feet, Andy's face reddened. "Whoa. That's the last time I touch any of Mrs. Gregg's lamb. It must have turned on me." He avoided eye contact, then glanced up at the lair's entrance. "Sorry I missed the show. What happened?"

Sean stared into the darkness. "Nothing. It looks like we're on our own now."

Andy turned to Sean. "What do you mean? Without Alexander's help?"

"It appears so. We better get back to see if Paladin is all right."

"Is that all you have to say? Alexander was our greatest hope, Sean!"

"He was a hope, but he cannot or will not help us. But Alexander is not our greatest hope. There is Another close by who is stronger and wiser. I have to believe He will make a way."

Sean turned to see the audience of dragons staring at them.

"This is just great!" Andy threw his hands up. "Now to finish off our little visit, Alexander probably gave them the signal that supper is now served."

"They won't bother us. Just walk slowly."

120

As the boys retraced their steps, a few dragons slid to the side to let them pass. Saber looked back and cast a long glance at the blue dragon, then followed Andy down the hill. The dragons watched the boys for a few minutes, then flew away one by one.

Clouds covered the sky now, and a light drizzle began to fall. Neither boy spoke on the way down the mountain. The mist felt cool against Sean's skin, red from the sun and exertion, and he inhaled the cool air. *Perhaps the king is mounting a grand rescue plan. Perhaps he already did, and Papa is home safe and sound.* But in the depths of his heart, Sean still felt the urgent need to follow through with his own plan.

By the time Saber flew them back to their departure point, they found Paladin resting where they had left him. Sean's legs ached, and he breathed hard. As he and Andy sat on a small boulder located under a tree near Paladin, Saber limped to Andy, who reached for Saber's feet. When he lifted them, he gasped. The rocky mountain had chipped and nicked Saber's scaly pads, and dark blood soaked their crevasses.

"How could I be such a fool, pushing him like I did! He's torn his pads."

Sean leaned over to look. "I'm so sorry, Andy."

"This is my fault," Andy said. "He was meant to fly, not trudge through rocks."

"Here, this will make him feel better." Sean poured water from his own flask over the dragon's pads. After emptying the flask, Sean set it

121

upright and then looked through his bag. He pulled out a shirt and tore it into strips. "Let's wrap these around his feet to provide some protection."

As they wrapped the strips around Saber's injured feet, Sean leaned down close to tie his strip. A hot gust of air blew his hair back, and the dragon pressed its smooth, silky nose against Sean's sunburned forehead. After a few seconds of snuffling Sean's hair, Saber flicked his red tongue across Sean's forehead.

Andy laughed. "He likes you."

"Yes, or he's trying to find out how I would taste." Sean licked his lips and tasted the salt of his sweat.

When they finished tending to Saber's injuries, the boys sat and stared into the distance. Andy pulled his hair back with both hands and looked down.

"I'm sorry, Sean. I just don't know if I can go on with you."

Sean nodded. "It's all right, Andy. I prepared for this. You have gone above and beyond the call of anything I asked you. You are a true friend for having stuck with me this long."

"Yeah, right, 'true friend.' I bloody well faint on you, and now I'm leaving you to finish your journey alone."

Sean shook his head. "Don't be silly; I don't look at it that way. Listen, when Saber feels good enough to fly, go back to the Greggs'. They wanted us to come back if we needed help and shelter. When this is over, I'll come for you. There will be a home waiting for you back in Maryport."

Andy looked up at Sean. "A home? Do you mean with you?"

"Of course I mean with me. My mother will love you."

"You mean your mother *and* your father." They smiled, and Sean nodded.

"Thank you, Sean. Thank you."

When Sean stood, Andy looked at him. "Are you sure you'll be all right on your own?"

Sean looked down. "Andy, I do not want you feeling guilty about this. Things could go badly. I've adopted you as my little—I mean, my younger brother. I would not want my younger brother to face the evil I may face. You would help me more if you returned to the Greggs and prayed for me. Will you do that?"

Andy looked away as his eyes filled with tears. He stood. "I will pray for you."

Compassion for Andy rose in Sean's heart, and he hugged the smaller boy. "Even with all the pain and heartache you've endured, I can see your heart always belonged to the Lord, and His love is healing you. And after a full, happy life, you will be reunited with your parents again." Sean added with a grin, "Just stay out of trouble until we meet again."

"I will do my best!" Andy chuckled. "How much farther do you have to go?"

Sean pulled out the map and hunched over it to protect it from any raindrops that might fall on it. "I'm not sure of the distance, so I'll just go north. I'll have to push Paladin to his limit, though. I feel like time is running out."

"You better go then; don't let us hold you back. Go in God's peace and protection, Sean. We'll meet again soon."

Hearing Andy mention God made Sean pause, then smile. "The same to you."

Sean gathered the reins and led Paladin back down the mountain. As the rain picked up force and drummed against his warm skin, he wondered if he would ever see his friend again.

# Chapter Twenty

When the showers subsided, the heavy clouds muted the sunset's brilliant colors. Since the rising moon could not illuminate Sean's travel into the night, he picked a secluded area in a grove of trees and searched for wood dry enough with which to build a fire. He peered under the trees and groped around to test the dampness of branches. Any cracking twig or rustling bushes made him jump, and he realized he hadn't appreciated Saber's presence until the dragon was no longer there to protect him.

Sean finally collected enough branches to create a modest blaze. As he pulled off his soaked sweater to dry by the fire, he felt grateful for the extra sweater Mr. Gregg had given him that he now pulled over his head. After securing Paladin near some tall grass, Sean pulled off the saddle and rummaged through his knapsack for food but found none. For the first time in his life, he would go to bed hungry.

Wrapping himself in damp blankets, Sean rested close enough to the fire for the heat to warm his face. Still, he shivered. Watching the sparks rise into the black sky, he wondered if Andy had made it back to the Greggs'. He imagined his young friend sitting in front of their fireplace with a bowl of shepherd's pie, regaling Victoria with their fearless exploits. The thought of Andy safe and sound made Sean smile.

With sleep embracing him, Sean thought of the other wonderful people he'd met along his journey. Micah's wisdom and warmth. Mr. and Mrs. Gregg's hospitality. And Victoria's kindness and beauty.

*She is beautiful.*

When Sean fell asleep, he dreamed of holding Victoria's hand as they walked through a sunny field of sweet-smelling flowers. They admired the tree-covered hills that rose up all around them and the sunshine that brought the colors to life. As they talked about the promises in the Bible, a warm breeze caressed the field.

As he turned towards Victoria to tell her how much their friendship meant to him, Paladin's whinny woke him. The last remnants of his dream faded, leaving a residue of frustration and longing. Yet he felt grateful that Paladin had wakened him early. As he looked up at the clear sky, the stars slipped under the horizon at one end of the skyline, and a sliver of the sun peeked above it at the other end.

After gathering his belongings and securing Paladin's saddle, Sean paused to pray for continued guidance. His stomach growled, but he had to move as fast as Paladin could carry him to the northern Cumbrian Mountains. Sean mounted the black horse, and they galloped with Sean's head held low to help them slice through the wind. Images from his dream flickered through his mind, and he forgot about his hunger.

\* \* \* \*

Mac awoke to the metal door slamming against the bars of their jail cell. The sun had not even risen and the familiar din of his fellow colliers had not yet begun. Eight tall guards entered the cell with swords drawn.

"Get down on the floor."

Disbrow folded his arms over his chest while Mac stared at the guards. Three leaped forward and seized Mac, while five tackled Disbrow. After they tied the men's wrists behind their backs with leather strips, the guards yanked them to their feet and shoved them out of the cell toward the main entrance.

As Mac passed through the main chamber where most of the laborers slept, he saw more guards brandishing their weapons. Crete, the black-haired guard behind Mac, broke the silence with a booming shout that made Mac flinch.

"Wake up!"

The other guards shouted too, and the laborers crawled to their feet with bleary eyes. Those who saw Mac and Disbrow looked down, their shoulders slumped. Mac lifted his chin, and before Crete turned back to him, he shouted too.

"It's all right, men! Be strong in your faith, and take courage. In the end, evil will never prevail over good."

127

Crete spun around and rushed to Mac, shoving him forward. Then, he called out to the other sentries. "After we leave, take every man outside to witness what happens to those who disobey!" He swept his eyes across the grime-streaked men who stood against the wall. "And if any of you blokes start acting brave out there, you will join these two as additional helpings for Nafaar's breakfast!"

As the guards laughed, a shout boomed from the back of the crowd, silencing their laughter. "Listen, to those who choose to hear!" The cavern grew quiet. The same voice rose again with gathering strength, "Psalm 34:17 says, 'Those who are right with the Lord cry, and He hears them. And He takes them from their troubles.'"

The familiar voice knocked the wind out of Mac. "No, Lord, please," he whispered.

Crete strode forward. "Show yourself if you have the courage!"

"Don't!" Mac shouted, receiving the back of a guard's hand across his face.

The crowd of laborers stepped aside as a man moved through the crowd. Erin strode forward, stopped within an arm's length of Crete, and folded his arms.

"Well, well," Crete said, glaring into Erin's blue eyes. "You are a brave one, aren't you?"

Erin glared back.

"Tether him!" Crete bellowed. "He will be Nafaar's dessert!"

The guards secured Erin, then pushed their captives forward again.

"Why, Erin?" Mac whispered. "You're throwing your life away!"

"Mac, you are the bravest, most honorable man I have ever met. It's an honor to lay down my life with you. Besides, those words from the Bible were burning in my heart. I felt compelled to proclaim them!"

Mac looked at his friend and gave a weak smile. "Has God given you any insight into our predicament and how He is going to deliver us?"

Erin chuckled. "Not yet."

# Chapter Twenty-One

Paladin's speed amazed Sean as trees and hills flew by. He wasn't sure how long he should drive Paladin this hard, but the stallion had barely broken a sweat. As they rode up a hill, Sean sensed someone watching them. When they reached the crest of the hill, he rested Paladin for a few minutes and scanned the countryside. Nothing but chirping birds. He shook off the feeling and nudged Paladin down the other side of the hill. As they moved down the incline, Paladin whinnied and stepped sideways. Sean tugged at the reins, struggling to regain control.

A shadow crossed the ground in front of them. Sean cast his eyes up to see the sun and sky obstructed by the underside of a huge grey dragon.

Paladin bolted down the hill and across the field at breakneck speed. Sean clung to the reins as the stallion's powerful haunches pumped beneath him. Heavy hooves pounded the grass, ripping up clods of dirt. As Sean struggled to breathe against the rushing wind, the dragon's shadow inched closer. He steered Paladin toward the dense forest ahead where the trees might afford some cover and he could try to take a stand against the dragon. Could he make it before the dragon caught him in its talons?

Seconds before they reached the shelter of the forest, a blinding pain struck Sean's sides as silver-plated talons closed around his waist. He clung to Paladin, but as the dragon pulled, the pain in his sides increased until he felt a faint ripping. Before he was torn in half, he released his hold and let the dragon lift him into the air. The forest below grew smaller as they rose, and the air grew thinner and colder. Black spots and stars swam before Sean's eyes.

A blur swept past them. The dragon stopped mid-air, making Sean swing forward and then dangle as the dragon hovered like an enormous humming bird. The blur flew past again, and the dragon's piercing shriek echoed through the sky. Sean looked up to see an arrow sticking out of its neck far above him.

"Sean, behind you!" a voice shouted.

*Andy!*

Sean craned his neck and looked back. Andy and Saber wheeled around behind the dragon, and Sean's heart raced.

The dragon swung around and blew a plume of fire. Saber darted out of the way like a fly dodging a swatting hand.

"Andy, what are you—"

Another volley of fire shot towards Andy and Saber, missing its mark by a millisecond.

131

Andy cupped a hand to his mouth and shouted. "I couldn't turn my back on my only friend! Can you pull yourself away? Saber will catch you!"

As the cat-and-mouse pursuit continued across the sky, Sean pried at the gigantic talons and wriggled without success. One talon pinned Sean's sword against him, and waves of nausea washed over him from the dragon's violent motions.

"It's no use, Andy!" Sean yelled. "Get away before you get hit!"

"The shofar, Sean! Drop the shofar! Saber will catch it!"

Saber darted to and fro, evading the bursts of fire as Sean pulled the leather strap from around his neck. As Andy guided Saber under the dragon, Sean took a deep breath and dropped the shofar.

The dragon holding Sean swung around and expelled a great fusillade of fiery missiles down at Saber and Andy. With not enough time to both catch the shofar and then escape the salvo of fire, Andy yanked the reins and pulled Saber down and away.

The shofar plummeted into the dense forest below.

When Sean stopped swinging long enough to dangle again, he scanned the sky for Saber or Andy. Nothing. Images of them lying on the forest floor tormented Sean, and his throat tightened. And Micah's shofar—gone forever.

As the dragon flew on, Sean realized where it was taking him. Less than an hour ago, Sean enjoyed the possible advantage of surprise in confronting the woman who kidnapped his father. Now he was being handed over to her with silver talons.

# Chapter Twenty-Two

s the guards led Mac and his friends out of the colliery and above ground, the sunlight struck Mac with blinding brilliance. The pain stabbed through the back of his eyes, and he jerked away and squeezed his eyes shut. He had not breathed the fresh air or seen the world beyond for some time now. A cool breeze blew across his face, and he actually relaxed a bit.

After a minute or two, Mac opened his eyes enough to squint through the bright light. About fifty meters from the colliery entrance stood a large wooden platform with two vertical posts. As the guards prodded them forward, long silvery-white hair and the blades of swords gleamed in the sunlight. Lady Silver, her two henchmen, Malek and Hector, and six guards stood waiting on the deck.

\* \* \* \*

As Sean hung from the dragon's talons, he decided God had bathed the powder-blue sky with sunshine today to prevent him from freezing to death. Violent winds whipped against Sean, making it almost impossible to open his eyes or take a deep breath. And then he caught the flash of a shining castle gleaming in the sunshine.

As the dragon descended, it stretched its wings and locked them into place, gliding for balance. Just before it crossed the peaks of the mountains, movement in the forest below caught Sean's attention. A large black form scaled the mountainside, but Sean could not tell if it was man or beast. When he looked up, he saw a throng of men gathered in front of what looked like a stage.

* * * *

The guards led Mac, Erin, and Disbrow up the platform steps as the rest of the captives emerged from the mine. Some men groaned and winced in the blinding sunlight – some of them had not seen daylight in more than a year. As the guards surrounded the miners, Lady Silver's legion of dragons watched them from the surrounding cliffs and trees.

Mac squinted up at the dragons. On his one side, the sun silhouetted their wings, and on his other side, it illuminated their gleaming scales. A larger dragon perched on a stone precipice above the rest, swaying back and forth. It, too, caught the light, which glinted from a silver spike on its forehead.

At first, Mac's breath caught in his throat. Then hot anger rushed through him as he remembered the dragon's icy grip, the ground dropping away, Cynthia and Sean's cries…

"Good morning, gentlemen," Lady Silver announced. "I trust you all slept comfortably."

A deep murmur grew among the men. Beside Lady Silver, Malek and Hector grinned.

"Quiet!" she shouted. "I see Crete exercised his discretion in adding another portion to the morning's menu. It appears we may have leftovers for Nafaar's little ones!" As she spoke, a wicked smile appeared, and she gazed up at the black dragon before looking back at the crowd.

Lady Silver swept an arm toward Mac, Erin, and Disbrow, then proclaimed, "I hereby pass judgment on these three men for lawless acts, and I condemn them to perish at the talons of Nafaar! Let this be a lesson to all who hear me!" She turned, then paused and stared into the sky.

A dragon approached, and in its talons dangled a person.

"Oh, how serendipitous!" She turned to Mac. "We've already found your replacement!"

Mac glared at her, but just before the dragon drew close enough to release its prey, a familiar voice reached Mac.

"Papa, Papa!"

*It can't be! He's home safe.*

The dragon released its captive, and the young man tumbled across the ground not far from the platform. *Windblown brown hair, hazel eyes—*

"No!" Mac screamed. He charged forward into two guards with enough power to knock them onto their backs as he leaped off the deck. When his feet hit the rocky ground, he could not reach out with his tethered wrists, so he tumbled across it. Behind him, Erin and Disbrow also threw themselves at the guards, hurling them off the platform.

Sean helped his father to his feet. Tears cut through the dirt on both their faces, and Sean hugged his father as Mac drew close enough to rest his forehead on his son's chest. Then Mac pulled away and stared at Sean, his mouth agape.

"Sean, what are you doing here?"

"The same thing you would have done!"

A guard shouted behind them. "Lady Silver, the slaves!"

Mac turned. The crowd of men pushed against the chain of guards.

"Secure them, or it will be your heads!" she screamed.

Two guards rushed at Sean and Mac. Before Mac could react, Sean unsheathed his sword and stood in front of his father, swinging the weapon.

"Stand back!" he roared. "Stay away from my father!"

As Sean threatened his assailants, the chain of guards shouted to the captives while jabbing their fingers at the dragons circling overhead. Within seconds, the captives settled, and even Erin and Disbrow allowed their guards to rush back onto the stage and seize them.

Lady Silver turned and fixed her devilish dark eyes on Sean. "Now, now, young man, let's all just settle down. Did I hear you say this man is your father?"

Without taking his eyes off the guards before him, Sean replied, "Yes, he is—and I will lay down my life defending him!"

"That is very honorable of you. And so you shall."

One guard in front of Sean pointed at the rust-colored blotches on Sean's blade and laughed. "What did you kill with that, boy? A fox?" The other guard sneered.

Sean snorted. "No, one of her dragons."

The guards exchanged looks, lifting their eyebrows.

Sean looked up at Lady Silver, who stared hard at him. "A green one, isn't that right? He's missing. Or did one of your men find his body already?"

Out of the corner of his eye, Sean saw the guards hush and steal a glance at Lady Silver. Her neck flushed a deep red and color rose to her cheeks. She glared down at Sean and Mac, and then looked behind her at Hector, a portly man with oozing pustules across his face.

"Hector, be a dear and shoot an arrow through this young man's heart. A guard will lend you a crossbow."

"No, please!" Mac cried out, darting in front of Sean. "Wouldn't he be more valuable to you in the colliery?" Behind his back, Mac wriggled his tethered wrists in front of Sean.

Before Lady Silver could respond, the sound of hooves striking against rocks reached them. A guard on horseback emerged from around the side of a hill. As he raced towards the platform, Sean lowered his sword and cut through the leather straps binding Mac's hands.

"I beg your pardon, your ladyship!" the guard shouted, "but the surveillance dragons are dead! Someone lured them with livestock roaming the outer fields. They ambushed our dragons and shot them full of arrows!"

"What? No!" Lady Silver stomped her foot against the wood. Turning, she slapped Hector upside the head. "What are you waiting for, you wart-covered toad! Shoot them both!" She gestured to Mac and Sean. "We have a colliery to secure!"

"Of course, Lady Silver!" Hector leveled his crossbow on Mac. As he lowered his eye to line up his sight, something struck his chest with a meaty *thok*. He gaped down at the tufted end of an arrow, and then stumbled forward. His knees folded beneath him and he crumpled to the platform.

Lady Silver's eyes widened. Her mouth dropped. Then she hurried down the steps, screaming, "The king's men are here! Take your positions! Malek, escort me to the castle!"

But Malek was nowhere to be seen.

"Where is that snake when I need him most!" she snarled at the nearest guard. "Crete, let's go!"

Thumping wings drowned out the guards' shouts as Nafaar and the dragons rose. Then flashes of red emerged from the surrounding hillsides, and the sounds of shouting and hoof beats filled the air. As Sean and Mac scanned the forest, dark shapes shifted among the trees and hundreds of arrows came flying at the dragons that swept in from all directions.

The captives rolled forward into the guards, and Mac and Sean rushed towards the platform to join Erin and Disbrow.

"Your mother, Sean … is she all right?" Mac asked as they neared the staircase.

"I'm sure she is, Papa; I've felt her prayers."

"Me too, son. Me too."

"Hurry, Mac!" Disbrow shouted, turning to show his bound wrists.

Two guards raised their swords at Mac and Sean, but a marksmen's arrow dropped one of them. Mac retrieved the sword from the corpse's hand before edging across the platform.

"Careful, Papa."

Mac charged and thrust the sword forward, but the guard backed up to within a meter of Disbrow. Mac locked eyes with the bearded captive and nodded. Before the guard could turn, Disbrow lifted his leg and kicked the guard in the back, sending him stumbling forward. Shifting his sword to his left hand, Mac swung his fist at the guard and struck him in the jaw. The guard tumbled over the edge of the platform and rolled to a stop on the ground, unconscious.

"It's about time, mate!" Disbrow grinned as Mac cut through the straps with the sword.

"My pleasure, Tiny," Mac replied as he turned to Erin.

A shadow fell across the platform.

"Watch out!" Sean shouted.

Nafaar dove at the cluster of men, his gleaming talons extended. Mac, Erin, and Disbrow ducked and dodged across the platform, but Sean screamed as the talons sank into his right arm. He seized the dragon's talons, but Nafaar rose until Sean's feet no longer touched the platform.

Mac rolled to his feet and charged the massive dragon with a raging cry. Lifting his sword, he aimed high above his son and plunged the blade through the dragon's thick scales into its leg. Nafaar's ear-splitting shriek drove Mac backward, his blood-smeared sword still lodged in the dragon's leg. Nafaar dropped Sean and rose into the sky.

"Get my son under the deck and protect him!" Mac said to Erin and Disbrow. "That black devil won't give up this easily!"

Erin and Disbrow pulled Sean to his feet, then guided him down the steps and under the platform. As Sean peered out from beneath the platform, dragons snatched some of the king's retreating men from their horses. By the colliery, the wall of guards pushed the unarmed captives back, and several dragons hissed and snapped at them. A large green dragon seized a captive and swung its head, flinging the man into the rock wall beside the colliery. The limp body rolled and fell, but the dragon caught it and tossed it into the air again before letting it hit the hard ground.

Sean's stomach rolled. He fought the bile rising in his throat.

Mac looked around the platform. His eyes fell on a crossbow and a quiver with only two arrows lodged under Hector's body. As Nafaar circled back around, Mac ran to the body, lifted its shoulder, and pulled the arrows from the surrounding pool of blood. Another guard rushed towards the platform with his sword drawn, but before he reached the staircase, Disbrow emerged from under the deck and tripped him.

Leaning over, Disbrow seized a step's wooden plank and ripped it off with a loud snapping and popping. Before the guard could get back to his feet, Disbrow struck him across the head and knocked him back to the ground. Then he looked up, his face red and streaked with sweat, and he smiled at Mac.

A blur whizzed by the platform, and Disbrow grunted and stumbled back, grimacing. An arrow stuck out of his upper chest. The bearded man fell to his knees.

"Tiny!" Mac yelled as he ran forward. "Erin, get out here and help him!"

As Erin sprinted forward, Mac raised his eyes to a guard approximately twenty meters away, the only one standing in front of the fight between the captives and the guards. Smirking, the guard placed another arrow across his bow.

Preparing his own bow, Mac dove to the platform floor, then rose up onto his knees and pulled the cord back. As the guard swung his crossbow up, Mac released his arrow. It punched clear through the man's chest, taking him to the ground.

Mac heaved a sigh and lowered his crossbow, shivering at the sudden realization that any number of marksmen could shoot him from where he stood in full view on the platform. He looked down at Erin crouched beside Disbrow, then rushed down the steps to Disbrow's side.

"Tiny, you're going to be all right. Let's get you under the platform."

"Can you help us get you up, Tiny?" Erin asked.

"I don't think it'll make any difference, mates," Disbrow said, pointing at the sky. "He's coming back."

Mac craned his neck and shielded his eyes from the sun. Nafaar, still high in the sky, descended toward them, and his shadow grew larger every second. Turning back to Disbrow, Mac leaned down and seized the man's upper arm. Erin followed suit, and the two men pulled Disbrow up and hurried him to the platform, where they tucked the wheezing man into the shelter beside Sean. As his son placed a hand on Disbrow's shoulder, Mac turned and ran back up the platform steps to grab his crossbow.

Standing in the center of the deck aiming the crossbow skyward, Mac noticed in his peripheral vision some of the king's men retreating. Mac's fellow captives were also losing ground in their battle to overpower the guards. It was not difficult to discern why. Lady Silver's army of dragons made this war virtually impossible to win. Simply put, they were outnumbered.

"Papa!" Sean screamed from under the platform. "Get down here and take cover!"

But Mac realized the platform provided only illusory protection; one blast of fire from Nafaar would turn it into an oven and incinerate them all. Mac grabbed his crossbow, fitted an arrow into it, and then ran down the stairs away from the platform. Nafaar screeched as he dove.

Mac pulled back the cord as far as it would stretch. As Nafaar thrust his talons forward, Mac took steady aim born of faith and held his breath.

Suddenly, a deep resonant blast pierced the air like a trumpet.

# Chapter Twenty-Three

Before Mac could release the arrow, Nafaar veered away, flapping like a startled bird. Sean emerged from under the platform and looked to the sky.

A huge dragon with gold scales across his massive chest shot over the mountains. Alexander pumped his wings in a flash of emerald green, and Sean jumped up and down.

"Papa, it's him! It's Alexander!"

From one end of the horizon to the other, Alexander's dragons filled the sky as they followed him into battle. And there, flying in formation with the rest, was Andy, riding Saber and blowing Micah's shofar with all his might.

Sean ran up the platform steps, tripping on one, and waved. "Andy! Down here!"

"Sean!" Mac motioned him back. "Get under cover!"

Sean ran back down the steps but kept his eyes on the sky. With Nafaar far from the platform, Andy and Saber landed next to it. Andy hopped off Saber and ran to Sean.

144

"You're alive!" Sean embraced his friend. "What happened to you and Saber? And the shofar! I thought we lost it!"

Andy grinned. "If only you could have seen how close we came to hitting the ground before Saber recovered!"

As they crawled under the platform, Sean asked, "How long did it take you to find the shofar?"

"A while because the forest was pretty thick, but thank God soon enough to get Alexander here in time." Andy looked at Mac. "Is this your father, Sean?"

"It sure is!" Sean flashed him a broad grin. "Papa, meet my friend Andy!"

"It's an honor, sir!" Andy shook Mac's hand.

Across from the platform, guards fled into the colliery as the captives and the king's men chased them. Dragons swept across the sky, their massive bodies and broad wings casting great shadows across the earth below. They clashed high above the platform where neither Mac nor Sean could see them, but their screams tore the air. Then Alexander came into view again as he circled in the sky above the colliery.

Nafaar appeared behind Alexander, his silver-plated spike flashing. With a powerful pump of his wings, the black dragon rose and then dove toward Alexander, extending his front talons.

"Look out!" Sean screamed, even though he knew the majestic dragon could not hear him.

Andy ran out from under the platform and brought the shofar's curve to his lips. As the trumpeting blast echoed beneath the platform, the men clapped their hands over their ears.

Alexander twisted in midair, catching sight of Nafaar. The black dragon slung his talons forward as far as he could, digging them into Alexander's back and slicing it as he careened sideways. Alexander rolled to face Nafaar with a piercing cry, but his maneuvering had kept the other dragon from lacerating the tendons near Alexander's wings.

A bright plume of fire streamed from Alexander's mouth, and as Nafaar twisted away, the flames scorched his wings. This time, his own shriek pierced the air, and black smoke rose from his singed membranes. Nafaar dropped a few meters, pumping his wings to stay aloft. In those seconds, Alexander pinned his wings to his side and plunged into Nafaar.

Mac gasped, and Sean and Andy cried out. Alexander bit into Nafaar's neck, and the other dragon's wild shriek weakened to a high-pitched whistle.

Erin cried out. "They're going to hit!"

But before the dragons reached the ground, Alexander sank his talons into Nafaar's sides, pulled his enemy up against him, and then hurled Nafaar down toward the earth. Nafaar's wings flailed as he fell, but Alexander spread his wings and rose away from the ground. The black dragon disappeared below the trees, his body twisted with his neck down.

The impact shook the ground with a loud boom, and an explosion of debris erupted on the horizon. Alexander swung low and blasted a steady stream of fire down at the spot where Nafaar hit. Within seconds, the faint sounds of popping and hissing reached the platform, reminiscent of logs in a campfire. The image of Nafaar's charred, smoking corpse appeared in Sean's mind.

Cheers erupted from beneath the platform as the men crawled out. Above them, the rest of Lady Silver's dragons pivoted in the middle of their flight and flew away. The cacophony of dragons in battle subsided, and only the beating wings and the calls of Alexander and his army broke the stillness.

Mac looked under the platform at Disbrow.

"We need to get Tiny a doctor, or we'll lose him. He's not making much sound, and last I checked, he's burning up." As Mac turned back to the others, the king's soldiers and the captives emerged from the colliery with the guards in tow, their wrists bound. Mac called out to them, "Do you have a doctor among you? We have a man who's badly hurt."

A member of the Royal Guard turned and shouted towards the soldiers, "Cooper!" Then he turned to Mac. "We have a medic on the way, sir."

"Thank you."

Sean scanned the area. Dozens of dragons lay dead or dying, their bodies lacerated or scorched, the vast majority belonging to Lady

Silver. As the remaining dragons disappeared from view, Alexander perched atop Lady Silver's castle.

"Look at him! He's huge!" Sean stared as Alexander spread his wings, the gold and emerald scales gleaming in the sun. Then, he stomped his right foot down onto a stone parapet, smashing it to pieces. He bellowed, and a great burst of fire shot from his maw.

In the field before the castle, a cadre of the king's soldiers approached with Lady Silver's guards in custody. Before they reached the entrance of the castle, the drawbridge lowered and the portcullis rose. Lady Silver emerged with Crete behind her, prodding her forward with his sword.

"Don't stick that thing into my back!" She glared at Crete. Then, reshaping her disheveled hair, she turned to the king's men. "Your king will not enjoy the last word in this matter! Where is Nafaar? Where is my dragon?"

"Lay down your sword!" a soldier ordered Crete. "And you, lady, keep your mouth shut!"

Crete stepped away from Lady Silver, tossed his sword to the side with a clang, and raised his hands.

A deep, elephant-like rumble emanated from Alexander, spreading across the land before him. He shifted his legs, then sprang into the sky and flew south. Mac and Sean watched until the dragon's silhouette faded into the distance.

# Chapter Twenty-Four

T he liberated captives embraced one another, and a few collapsed to their knees, looking into the sky and thanking God for their freedom. From the ocean of voices swept word that the Royal Guard would march the prisoners to England's highest security prison near Blackburn to await sentencing from the king.

As Mac and Sean stood beside the platform, an older man with salt and pepper hair rushed over. "I am Cooper. Where is the injured man?"

Mac pointed under the platform where Erin attended to Disbrow, who lay unconscious. As the medic ran under the platform, one of the king's Royal Guard walked up to Andy and extended his hand. Dressed in a striking uniform of bright red and blue with gold epaulets, the bearded man towered over the boy.

"I'm Captain Waterford. Are you the young man who brought Alexander here?"

Craning his neck, Andy returned the handshake with an awestruck smile. "Yes, sir."

"The king will want to meet you. Can you accompany us back to London?"

"Wha—well, uh … I don't—"

Sean placed his hand on Andy's shoulder. "He will be honored to, sir."

Andy stood with an open mouth for a moment, then looked at Sean and then back to the captain. "Sir, Sean here is really the one responsible for Alexander coming to help."

The captain turned to Sean. "Is that true, son?"

Mac stood behind Sean, listening with a proud grin.

Sean flushed. "Well, sir, I guess you could say both Andy and I convinced Alexander."

"Then the king will want to meet you both," the captain declared. "Can you join us?"

Sean looked back at his father, who shrugged. "It's up to you, son."

"Captain, I hope this won't appear disrespectful," Sean said, "but I really want to go home to see my mother first. And I need to find my horse, Paladin. And maybe stop to see some friends who helped us during our journey—if it's all the same to you, sir."

Mac looked down at Sean with a puzzled expression.

"That's fine," the captain replied, "but can you young men promise me you will visit His Majesty as soon as you can?"

"Yes, sir," they replied.

The boys shook the captain's hand, and as the captain mounted his horse, Mac approached him. "Captain, we are extremely grateful for your service."

"You're welcome, sir, but it appears we all need to thank these two boys."

Mac nodded, smiling.

"And incidentally," the captain added, "we have several wagons of food and blankets and some horses on their way, courtesy of the king. You all may need to double up on the horses, but they should help everyone get home. Good luck."

"Thank you again, Captain. God be with you on your journey back."

The captain tipped his hat and trotted off. His soldiers followed with Lady Silver, Crete, and the guards shackled and on foot.

Mac walked back to Sean. "Who are these friends you told the captain about?"

"It's a long story, Papa. I'll tell you on the way home."

When Mac and Sean walked back to the platform, Cooper the medic emerged. "It's hard to say how this will turn out for him. I'm very concerned about his high fever." He shook his head. "I'm not adequately equipped to treat him here. I think it would be best for him to return with us, but we have a long way to travel. He's awake, though, and he wants to talk to you."

Thanking the doctor, Mac knelt beside his friend. "The doctor tells me you'll be ready for more adventure tomorrow, Tiny."

"I doubt that, mate." Disbrow's voice did not rise above a whisper, and he struggled to breathe. "Listen, Mac, if things don't turn out—"

"Don't talk like that, Tiny."

"I know, I know." His breathing grew more labored. "But just in case it don't turn out so good, I need you to do something for me."

"All right."

"Will you go see my father in Whitehaven and tell him … I love him and … I forgive him?"

Mac's jaw quivered, and he looked at the ground.

"Will ya, Mac?"

"Yes, Tiny."

"Thank you. And one more thing, Mac." Disbrow's eyelids drooped under the weight of fatigue. "Will you tell him about Jesus?"

"We'll both tell him." But Disbrow's eyes had fluttered shut, and his chest rose and fell with quiet breaths. "We'll both tell him, Tiny."

After giving Disbrow's arm a gentle squeeze, Mac stepped out from under the platform and walked to the medic. "Can you get a few men to place him on a wagon?"

Cooper nodded. "Of course."

After the Royal Guard left with the prisoners, the king's attendants arrived with horses and wagons filled with provisions: meat and vegetable pies, roast beef and lamb, Yorkshire pudding, green beans, Cornish pasties, even freshly smoked fish and apples picked along the way. Having tasted nothing but bland porridge for every meal, the captives ate until their stomachs swelled.

After their heavy meal, most captives fell asleep in the back of the wagons or curled up in the grass. When Mac and Sean awoke, the groggy men around them hugged one another and said their goodbyes before setting out for home. From among the crowd, Erin approached Mac. The men embraced, then Mac put his hands on the man's shoulders.

"If you ever visit Maryport, stop by for a cup of tea," he said.

"Thank you, Mac; I'll do that. I'm honored to call you my friend."

"Likewise." Mac smiled and stepped back. "Go in God's peace and protection."

Then Erin looked at Sean and shook his hand. "Take good care of your father."

Within minutes, Erin rode off with a partner travelling in the same direction. When Sean turned to his father, Andy stood behind him chewing on a lamb shank.

Sean laughed. "Why am I not surprised you're still eating?"

"All this fighting makes me hungry," Andy said with his mouth full.

Sean looked around. "Where's Saber?"

Andy turned and pointed over his shoulder. In one of the wagons, Saber scavenged what little food remained. Andy chuckled. "Poor fellow. He needs some big, plump fish!"

"Andy, where do you live?" Mac asked.

Before Andy could answer, Sean spoke up, "Well, Papa, Andy doesn't have a home or a family. I thought if—"

"You're welcome to stay with us, Andy," Mac said, "but the dragon—"

Sean placed his hand on his father's arm. "Papa, you know, that's how I felt when I first met Saber, but you'll love him. He won't hurt a soul!"

"I'm not worried about our souls, Sean; I'm worried about our livestock!"

"Trust me, Papa, he won't touch them. He likes fish."

Mac studied Andy's crestfallen expression. "All right, boys, but the first time he—"

Andy's eyes lit up, and he grabbed Mac's hand, shaking it. "There won't be a first time, Mr. Delbridge! I promise! Thank you, thank you!"

Wrestling his hand back after a moment, Mac placed his hands on his hips. "Now, how are we going to do this? Us on horseback and Andy on … dragon-back?"

An attendant approached Mac. "Do you blokes need more horses and a wagon?"

"That's the ticket!" Andy snapped his fingers. "Saber could ride in luxury!"

"You don't need it, sir?" Mac asked.

"The Royal Guard already took the wagons they needed, and we set aside the ones we need, so help yourself. I'm sure the king won't mind helping our heroes."

Andy saluted the soldier. "Thank you so much, sir."

"You're welcome." The soldier left and returned with a horse and wagon in tow.

Mac grabbed the reins. "Sean, you and Andy pilot the wagon. I'll ride the horse."

Saber curled up in the wagon bed, wrapped his wings around himself, and fell asleep. With a clear sky and cool breeze at their backs, the party rolled away, leaving the blood-soaked land and the colliery behind them.

"Papa, want to try the best cherry pie you'll ever eat?" Sean asked.

"You mean your mother's pie?"

"Well, the second best, then." Sean turned to Andy. "But don't tell Victoria I said that."

"Victoria? Who's Victoria?"

"She is the sweetest, most beautiful—"

"Here we go." Mac chuckled.

"Wait till you meet her, Papa!"

# Chapter Twenty-Five

The following afternoon, the wagon rolled through the field where the dragon had seized Sean. As he gazed across the grass, his eyes stung with tears. Lady Silver's dragons had frequented these lands, and they probably ate whatever large game they could find. A horse lost in the midst of hungry dragons …

As they topped the crest of a hill, Mac let out a surprised exclamation. Sean turned to see a black stallion grazing near the forest's edge.

"Paladin!"

The horse looked up with perked ears, then tossed his head and whinnied. Sean jumped off the wagon and sprinted toward Paladin. As he threw his arms around the horse's neck, Paladin snuffled the boy's hair and nickered.

"You're safe!" Sean inhaled the scent of hot horse fur and pressed his face against Paladin's neck. After checking him for wounds, Sean attached Paladin to the wagon beside his father's horse, then realigned Paladin's saddle and climbed up into it. Every few minutes during the rest of their journey, Sean leaned down and patted the horse's neck.

The next day, they arrived at the Greggs' and spent the evening sharing their stories and enjoying cherry pie. When Sean pried his eyes from Victoria, he caught his father's gaze. Mac smiled and nodded; not only was the pie delicious, but Victoria was—next to Cynthia—the loveliest young lady he had ever met.

When they left the next morning, Mac mounted his horse, and Andy climbed into the wagon bed to curl up on a blanket under Saber's insulating wing.

Sean shook Victoria's hand. "I promise to write."

Victoria smiled and looked at the ground. "I hope we see you again soon."

Mac cleared his throat twice before Sean left Victoria to mount Paladin.

\* \* \* \*

After two more days of rugged travel, they arrived at Micah's grotto. During the introductions, Sam growled and circled Saber from a distance, his hackles bristling from neck to tail. Easily four times the wolf's size, Saber sat back on his haunches like a dog and watched the wolf with his lustrous blue eyes. When Sam made a small rush at the dragon, Saber flung his wings wide with a burst of air. The wolf snarled and sprang away, then turned and glared at him.

Andy and Micah laughed. Sam ignored them and glanced back at Saber as he padded to Paladin, pawing at his old friend. When they entered Micah's grotto, Mac and Andy marveled at its comfort and beauty before sitting down to dinner. They enjoyed Micah's trout while he told them about his experience finding Sam and meeting Sean.

Mac and Micah spent the rest of the evening discussing their adventures and how grateful they were for God's help. Before bed, Sean approached Micah with the shofar; a small scratch down one side made Sean's stomach quiver. But before he could open his mouth, Micah smiled and shook his head.

"This is your shofar now, Sean. I think God wants you to have it."

Knowing better than to argue, Sean smiled and tucked it into his knapsack. "Thank you, Micah. Your—the shofar saved everyone. Papa, me, the colliers, the king."

Micah nodded and smiled.

The next morning, Mac and Micah joined each other praying for protection. As the party set out on the final leg of their journey home, they passed the clearing where Prince trotted behind the great white wolf, following Sam wherever he went.

During the rest of the trip, the clouds returned but without rain. As the wagon rolled down the streets of Maryport that evening, not a single soul appeared. Moving farther through the village, the party approached the church. Lit candles rested on the sills of the windows, and hymns emanated from within its walls.

Mac turned to Sean. "I wonder if your mother is in there. I don't think the news of our freedom would have reached here yet."

"Let's go see, Papa. Can you imagine her surprise when she sees us?" Sean grinned.

"Can you imagine her surprise when she sees this dragon?" Mac glanced back at Saber, then climbed off his horse. "Let's take a look inside."

"Stay, Saber." Andy draped several blankets over the dragon, then hopped down. Sean looked at the shifting pile of blankets and back to Andy, who shrugged. "Better to hide him in case someone sees him."

Climbing the church's wooden steps, they opened the doors, but the enthusiastic hymn-singing drowned out the squeak of the hinges, so no one knew that the travelers had entered. Andy stayed at the back of the church while Mac and Sean walked down the main aisle, smiling as their friends and neighbors turned and stared at them. Each row fell silent when they passed. As they neared the front, Vicar Perry looked up from his hymnal and stared, mouth open.

Sean's mother sat in the front row, singing from her hymnal. Mac pursed his lips and pressed his forefinger to them, looking up at Vicar Perry. As the voices dwindled, only a handful of people with their backs to them still sang. Soon everyone—including Sean's mother—stopped singing. She looked up at the vicar.

"Cynthia," Mac whispered.

She gasped.

"Mama," Sean said. "We're home."

She spun around in her seat, saw them, and brought her hands to her mouth. As she stood, a sob burst from her. She rushed to Mac, stretching out an arm to pull Sean to her as well. The family broke down in tears and clutched one another as the rest of the onlookers cheered until the old stained glass windows rattled.

When Mac and Sean let go of Cynthia, Andy appeared standing behind them. The crowd pressed in around them while Sean introduced Andy to his mother, then to the rest of the people. When Sean looked back to Andy, the boy's beaming smile and glistening eyes told him Andy was finally home.

* * * *

Ten days later, Mac sat down with Sean and Andy as they sipped tea.

"I received a message from Dr. Cooper," he said with a sigh. "Tiny died during the middle of that first night." He looked down and blinked back tears.

"I'm sorry, Papa," Sean said in a quiet voice. "At least we know where he is and that he is happy."

The words lifted Mac's heavy thoughts. He smiled and nodded. Two days later, he made the journey alone to Whitehaven to see Tiny's father as he had promised. Upon hearing of his son's death, Mr. Disbrow opened his mouth and sat down, staring at the ground.

Mac sat beside the man and explained how his son had helped bring Lady Silver to justice. "He was—he is a hero." Mac also told Mr. Disbrow about Tiny's decision to give his heart and life to God and he now rested in Heaven. Mr. Disbrow shook his head when Mac offered to pray with him before he left, but the man promised to think about returning to church.

\* \* \* \*

The citizens of Maryport treated Mac, Sean, and Andy to smiles, greetings, and occasional discounts and dinners with neighbors. But, at last, life on the farm resumed. Andy helped Sean with chores, and the boys read the Bible together every evening before bed. When Saber was not fishing at sea, or in nearby streams and lakes, he followed the boys everywhere they went and often stood watch over the sheep like a faithful dog. Visitors shied away when they first met him, but soon he gained the town's affection, and several people visited just to see a dragon in the flesh.

\* \* \* \*

And finally, after many battles, hardships, and unknowns and after living only on hope and trust in God, this particular story ends on an unusually warm April morning with Andy astride Saber soaring through the skies. This sight would not present any irony, in particular, were it not for the fact that Sean sat behind him, strapped on and screaming for dear life.

Andy learned there was only one thing that would get Sean on the back of a dragon and hopefully break his fear of flying.

They were on their way to see Victoria.

# End

# Acknowledgements

First and foremost, I am grateful to my precious Lord, Savior, and King, Jesus Christ, for giving me this story.

My thanks also to—

My wife, Cindy, who supported me throughout this project. You are the best!

My gifted brother, Steve Wolf, who provided the wonderful artwork on the cover and back of the book. You can find him at http://www.wolfcreativeusa.com.

To three peerless editors at Inspiration for Writers—

- Sandy Tritt, CEO of the online service Inspiration for Writers (www.inspirationforwriters.com), who proved to be an indefatigable source of counsel throughout this project. *Always* there when I needed her.

- Jessica Murphy, without whose assistance this book would not have seen the light of day.

- Wendy Chorot, the first professional voice who told me to "go for it!"

Susanne Wilson, a good friend and sister in Christ, whose wise godly counsel and assistance proved invaluable. I could not have done it without you!

Family, friends, and pastors help to shape who we are and what we become in life. While it would require copious amounts of ink to create a list of all my precious children and their spouses, beautiful grandchildren, siblings, nephews, nieces, in-laws, cousins, aunts, uncles, and friends who have been such a blessing to me; suffice it to say that each one of you is a gift from God.

To my parents, Fred and Peggy Wolf — As patriarch and matriarch of the Wolf clan, your Christ-centered counsel has helped all your children through many storms. Thank you, Mom and Dad!

God bless you all!

# Alexander
## The Good Dragon

AlexanderTheGoodDragon.com

CPSIA information can be obtained at www.ICGtesting.com
Printed in the USA
LVOW11s0737290515

440388LV00002B/2/P

9 780692 441619